ALT ED

ALT ED

CATHERINE
ATKINS

G. P. PUTNAM'S SONS • NEW YORK

For their help with this book, my gratitude to Shirley Harazin,
Amanda Jenkins, Ann Manheimer, Martha Moore,
Mary Pearson, and Dona Vaughn.

My thanks to Kathy Dawson for her ideas and suggestions,
to Ginger Knowlton for her belief in this book, and
to Kelly Going for her enthusiasm.

Copyright © 2003 by Catherine Atkins
G. P. PUTNAM'S SONS,
a division of Penguin Putnam Books for Young Readers,
345 Hudson Street, New York, NY 10014.
G. P. Putnam's Sons, Reg. U.S. Pat. & Tm. Off.
Published simultaneously in Canada. Printed in the United States of America.
Designed by Carolyn T. Fucile. Text set in Bulmer.
Library of Congress Cataloging-in-Publication Data
Atkins, Catherine. Alt ed / Catherine Atkins. p. cm.
Summary: Participating in a special after-school counseling class
with other troubled students, including a sensitive gay classmate,
helps Susan, an overweight tenth grader, develop a better sense of herself.
[1. Behavior—Fiction. 2. Interpersonal relations—Fiction.
3. High schools—Fiction. 4. Schools—Fiction.] I. Title.
PZ7.A862 Al 2003 [Fic]—dc21
2002016942
ISBN 0-399-23854-9
3 5 7 9 10 8 6 4 2

To my mother, Liz Bass

Contents

1
KALE KRASNER TAKES MY RULER

Freshman year, spring

THE MAGAZINE I WANT IS IN THE RACK BEHIND ME. I reach around to grab it. That is all the time Kale Krasner needs. When I turn back, he is sitting across from me, and my ruler is gone.

"Hey there," he says, grinning.

"Hi, Kale." My voice cracks on his name.

"You working on that report thing?"

"Yes," I tell him, looking at the place my ruler used to be. "I was drawing a map. A map of Brazil."

"Cristy's doing the map at our table. Ecuador, wherever that is. Why aren't you working with a group, like everyone else?"

I blink at him. "I need my ruler to finish the map."

Kale shakes his head. "You left your ruler lying out where anyone could take it. You need to learn to take better care of your stuff."

I look at him. I don't bother to look for the teacher, Mrs. Warren.

"Did you take my ruler?"

Kale nods. Once. Slowly. My stomach tightens.

1

"Can I have it back?"

"No. What would that teach you?"

I gather my books, the *Time* magazine, my half-finished map, notebook, and pen.

"I have to make copies," I say to the air, past Kale's chuckle.

Walking away, I am hyperconscious of my every bulge and jiggle as he takes in the back view. In front I clutch my stuff tightly as if I am fording a flooded river.

I pass table after table of students who want nothing to do with me. I hear a few stifled laughs, several variations of the word *fat*, and one pitying *Just look at her.*

At the front counter the librarian, Ms. Henderson, is chatting with Mrs. Warren. They continue their conversation until I clear my throat.

"Susan, it's not time to check out books," Mrs. Warren says.

"I know. I was wondering if I could copy an article." I try to extricate *Time* from the rest of my things. It slides through my fingers, taking my notebook with it to the floor. I stumble a little, trying to hold on. The chatter in the library lessens, replaced by scattered giggles and someone's grunt as I stoop to retrieve the drops.

"Go ahead, Susan," Ms. Henderson says, pushing back her heavy hair. "In there." She gestures toward the L-shaped room behind the counter.

Inside I take several deep breaths, eyes closed, my stuff piled on the copy machine. I know my face is red, that every word I have spoken in the last five minutes has emerged trembling. And I know that I am taking things too hard, making a fuss over simple events no one else much cares about. Knowing this does not help.

When I open my eyes, I see a movement off to the side. Before I can stop myself, I gasp.

"It's okay. Just me." A thin, brown-haired boy steps out from an alcove to the left of the copy machine. He is holding a sheaf of magazines.

"Do you need to make copies?" I ask. "I can go . . . somewhere else."

"No." He waves a hand at me. "I was sorting these in the periodicals room. I saw you out here and just thought I'd say hi."

"Hi." I collect myself, ready for the joke.

"I'm Brendan Slater. I work in the library. I've seen you here before."

"Uh-huh." I look at him, waiting.

"Did something happen out there?" All at once Brendan is searching me. "You look so . . ." He hesitates.

"So ugly," I say, then turn away, appalled.

"No. That's not what I was going to say. Sad, maybe."

Who is he to tell me I am sad? I pick up *Time* and shuffle through it, trying to look busy.

"They go after me too, is all."

I stop what I am doing. "Who says anyone was going after me?"

Brendan shrugs. "I've seen that look before."

I wonder how much he has seen—and heard. "You felt sorry for me."

"Maybe. Not in a bad way."

"There is no good way to feel sorry for someone."

"Sure there is."

"Kale Krasner took my ruler." I hold my breath, waiting for Brendan's reaction. It is late in coming. "I don't mean you should do something about it, or anything like that. But that's what happened."

Brendan leans against the door frame. "Kale Krasner is demented."

I allow myself a small grin. "I didn't think anyone but me noticed."

He raises his eyebrows. "I saw him once in Building A kicking the wall over and over, all by himself. He didn't know anyone else was around."

"Really?" I lean against the copy machine, interested. "He's always doing these weird things to me. Like first day of English, he grabs my notebook, rips out a page, then just stares at me. Like I'm going to scream or cry or something."

"It almost sounds like he likes you," Brendan says, and I shut down, turning back to the copier.

"Yeah, that must be it," I say, as close to bitchy as I dare.

"Did I say something wrong?" Brendan asks after a few seconds of silence.

"You weren't making fun of me just now? Saying Kale Krasner 'likes' me?"

"No. No way. What's your name?"

"Susan Callaway." I turn back, trying to remember where I've heard his name before. Somewhere. "You said people get after you. Why would they?" Brendan is average-looking, almost handsome, lean, with a tennis player's build.

"You don't know about me?"

"No. I'm pretty out of it." I smile a little.

"You must be." Brendan is thoughtful. Then a grin busts free and moves him from okay-looking to really cute.

We are quiet, looking at each other.

"You check out film books a lot, don't you?" he says. "I see your name in the records."

I squint at him. "Scripts, yeah. I like movies."

"I love them." He is solemn. I nod.

At the same moment, each of us turns away.

"I have to get back to work," Brendan murmurs.

"Yeah, me too." I take up copying, closing the lid a little too hard with each new page. I am working to keep the smile off my face. A successful human encounter.

———

AT HOME MY BROTHER TOM FILLS ME IN ON Brendan Slater. He wrote a love letter to another boy. He was caught kissing his best friend. He looks at other guys in the locker room. He meets men in the park after school. The entire sophomore class is boycotting him. Brendan Slater is the school freak.

"Watch out," Tom says. "Watch out or that will be you."

2
Starting It

Sophomore year, spring

MR. DUFFY IS SMILING. BEAMING. AT ME. ROY DUFFY, aka Puffy, Doofy, Doofdork, and Lardass. Head counselor at Wayne High; campus joke. I can't look away from the tooth stained gray in his lower jaw.

"I took a punch there," he says. "Back when I was teaching."

"Sorry." I switch my view to my clasped hands and see by my watch that it is almost time for a class change. Mr. Duffy's office faces the Wayne High courtyard and his blinds are up. The window is smoked, but still . . . I don't want anyone to see me. I don't want anyone to know. "Mr. Duffy," I say, "can you . . . ?"

"I asked the kid to put out his cigarette and wham! Can you believe that?"

He wants to talk about himself. I smooth my face into a mask of interest. "That's terrible," I say. "Was the kid expelled?"

Mr. Duffy regards me for a moment. "What do you accomplish by expelling a kid? Nothing. Expulsion means giving up. I'm all about trying."

A nod seems called for, so I give him one. Tentatively, I point to the blinds. "Mr. Duffy, I wonder if—"

"That's why you're here, Susan, in my office, not the vice principal's. Kids like you are too valuable to waste."

I nod, resigned, giving up on the blinds. Mr. Duffy is wrong. I am here, in his office, because my dad coaches football for Wayne High. Varsity football, Valley Oak League champs three years running. That's why I'm here.

"I've asked around about you," Mr. Duffy says. "Your teachers couldn't stop raving. So bright. So intelligent. They love you."

I shrug. They don't know me.

"When I asked about friends," he says, "none of your teachers could come up with any. Do you have friends?"

"Yes," I begin, but my throat closes and I double-clutch a swallow. He watches and waits. "I have all the friends I need."

"Do you?" he says, eyes searching. "Do you really?"

I want to laugh in his face. Instead I change the subject. "Mr. Duffy, I'm here because of the thing with the truck. Tell me what I have to do, and I'll do it, but please, don't ask about personal things."

Don't ask me about friends.

"You think this is a one-time visit, Sue?"

"It's Susan," I say, my voice soft but firm.

"Susan, then." He leans forward, meaty hands gripping the edge of his desk. "I'm starting a group. I want you in it. Your attendance is the payment for what you did."

"My attendance?" I stare at him. "You mean, I have to come back here?"

A smile tugs at one side of his mouth. "Not here. The group is going to meet in the Vocational Ed trailer. Every Wednesday afternoon, three-thirty to four-thirty, for the rest of the semester."

Too much to take in. I fasten on the worst part. "A group? You mean, other people?"

Oh yeah, Susan, you're so smart.

"Yes," he says. "This group is going to take the place of expulsion for a number of people. Six of you, in fact."

"You want me to sit there with a bunch of kids who should have been thrown out of school?"

"Yes, Susan." Mr. Duffy's eyes are mild. "That's one thing you'll all have in common."

"I don't need a group," I say. I even smile at him. His expression doesn't change. "Can't we just talk, you and me?"

Great. Now I'm begging to be counseled. By this counselor.

"A group is exactly what you need," Mr. Duffy says. He steeples his hands, nodding. "You need people. You need friends."

I picture it, me spilling off my chair, sitting in a circle with five wanna-be gangsters. Staring at my lap while they laugh at me.

"Mr. Duffy," I start, but I can't think of a thing to say to change his mind about me.

He's beaming again. "This is the first time the administrators have agreed to sponsor a group like this. I've been asking for years. This could be the start of a great tradition at Wayne High. Can I count you in?"

"You don't have to waste time convincing me," I tell him. "My dad says I'm in, I'm in."

"I haven't wasted my time, dear." Mr. Duffy's voice is so unexpectedly kind, the "dear" doesn't bother me. "I've enjoyed our talk."

8

The bell rings, shatteringly loud. Across the courtyard I see a row of doors flung open and students pouring out. I know the same thing is happening on our side.

"Mr. Duffy," I say, leaning forward, "can you lower the blinds, please?"

"Hmm?" He peers at me. "Yes, of course."

Mr. Duffy shifts around for the cord, trying to reach it from his chair. Too late: Kale Krasner and Jason Schrader are at the window, hands cupped to see who is being counseled.

Kale's mouth stretches into an exaggerated grin as he recognizes me. "Don't cry, baby!" he shouts, tugging at Jason's shoulder as Mr. Duffy stands, blocking the boys until the blinds can do the job.

"I'm sorry, Susan," he says, his back to me. I can't read his voice.

Outside I am wary, but Kale and Jason have gone. I join the stream, ready, head down, face expressionless. Inside I am considering Kale. He is even dumber than I thought. I never cry at school. Never. No one knows that better than him.

———

Sunday dinner at Denny's with Dad, and my brother isn't here.

"You screwed up, Susie," Dad says. "And now you have to pay."

I nod, afraid to look at him. Then I do, but Dad isn't looking at me. He is fiddling with his playbook, with the thick rubber bands that hold the book together, his gaze unfocused on the tabletop between us.

"I'm sorry, Dad. Really sorry."

"The principal's agreed to keep this quiet, as long as you do your

part. I paid for the truck, for what you and that other kid did. The owner thinks the school took care of it."

I cringe. "Really sorry."

"You're going to pay with your time," Dad says. "I want you to see Roy Duffy tomorrow. I set you up with an appointment. He'll tell you what you have to do."

"Mr. Duffy?" I wrinkle my nose. "You mean the counselor at Wayne High?"

"See him tomorrow," Dad tells me. "First thing in the morning. Do what he says to make this right."

The thickest rubber band snaps against Dad's fingers and he pulls his hand back with a mild curse. Our eyes meet. Dad tilts his chin at me, waits till I nod. Then he's gone, looking past me at nothing, at the darkness outside the restaurant, the headlights and taillights passing by.

The waitress swings by, pen ready. She's new.

"What can I get you folks?"

Dad brightens, opening the menu and pointing to the steak platter. Baked potato, bleu cheese, more coffee.

"And for you, ma'am?"

That's me. Ma'am. The waitress is at least twice my age.

"I'll have the same," I tell her, my hunger driving me past the insult. At home I cook, or Dad stocks up on Stouffer's frozen dinners. Denny's means real food once a week.

"Except not coffee," I add. "A Coke."

"Miss, make that a Diet," Dad says. The waitress smiles. She's not young, but she has a young body. I don't.

This time it is me who looks away.

I ARGUE WITH MYSELF AS I PACE THE WALK TO French II. Dad couldn't have known about Mr. Duffy's group. He couldn't have wanted me to talk about myself, or anything else, with a bunch of strangers.

You do what he says to make this right.

That's as close as Dad has come to talking about what I did. What he *thinks* I did.

"Look at her," someone says, and that's when I see the boys. There are five of them. Jocks, maybe, but not first string. One is my brother Tom. They stand in a loose circle at the top of the stairs leading down to my next class. I can take another flight of stairs if I double back. Useless: They have already seen me. Nothing to do but move forward.

"Hey, honey, hey, babe," one croons, glancing around the circle.

"He wants your body," another says, pushing a skinny blond my way. The blond, cackling, holds up his fingers in the sign of the cross.

"Not that, anything but that," he moans. He is ugly, major ugly, but they so often are.

Tom is in the middle of the circle, looking embarrassed. His friend Scott, the only other boy I recognize, steps into my path. We are not friends, but we know each other. I see him some mornings when he comes by for Tom.

"Hi, Susan," he says loudly. Loud for effect? "How's it going?"

I don't know if I should respond. Scott looks earnest; the other guys are rolling their eyes, snickering, elbowing each other. My brother is staring at the ground.

"Hi, Scott," I say, and move a slow sidestep past. He nods and blends back into the circle.

"That's Tom's sister," I hear him say behind me. I don't hear anything after that, and I try to push the boys out of my mind as I descend the stairs.

If Tom's friends had been coming on to me because they thought I was pretty, he would have been the one to stop them, not Scott. He would have been proud to say he was my brother. But I am fat, and because of that all bets are off.

3
PREGAME

ON THE FIRST DAY OF MR. DUFFY'S GROUP I'M AT
the Vocational Ed trailer at three-thirty. I try the knob—stuck
fast—then step up to peek into the chicken-wired trailer window.
Inside it's dark, empty. Nobody else is here. Spotlighted in bright
sunlight on the wobbly metal platform, I shuffle, I curse, and I
wait.

A sadist couldn't have picked a better spot. Voc Ed is in the
heart of Wayne High's outdoor athletic complex. The tennis
courts are directly across from the trailer; in a few weeks the courts
will be filled with green-shorted, shirtless boys batting the ball
around for practice. But today the courts are empty.

From the other side of the trailer I hear the calls and groans of
Wayne High baseball players taking the track, Coach Linder
screaming them on. My brother is out there among them. My
cheeks burn thinking of what those boys would be saying to me
without the protection of Voc Ed's crackerbox walls.

"Callahan, quit doggin' it!" someone yells, so fast, so close, I
think they are calling me. I flatten my body against the paint-
splintered brown door, tensed for the next jab.

13

Two facts register, and my heart slows. The voice came from the field—some jock message—and it was meant for Calla*han,* not Calla*way.*

I stand up straight, my books clasped to my chest. I even smile a little. I know who Callahan is, and I can picture him jogging. A pleasant sight.

"Get out here with us, you lazy bastard," the same voice calls, fading out on *bastard,* and Randy Callahan steps into view from the alleyway between the Special Ed and Voc Ed trailers.

He raises a hand against the sun and looks left, then right, stopping when he sees me. I take a sudden and desperate interest in the tops of my sneakers. Watching Randy Callahan is my favorite pastime; being watched by him is unprecedented.

Relax. Randy Callahan is not in this group. He couldn't be. He's passing by, on the way to somewhere else.

"This where Duffy's group meets?" Randy is in front of the platform now, his voice friendly, deep.

I raise my head, stunned, not taking in his exact words. He holds my look a moment, then shrugs.

"That counseling thing?" he says. "This is Voc Ed, right?"

I realize I am blocking the sign. Stepping forward, I gesture at the door. "Yeah, this is Voc Ed, and he said . . . so I guess this is the place."

"Great." Randy climbs the four steps and settles on the top one, facing away from me. I wait for him to say more, but then I remember that for Randy I do not exist. The knowledge comes as a comfort.

Safe now, almost happy, I take in the back of his head. A familiar sight, the touchstone of my day.

Randy is Callahan to my Callaway, and at Wayne High teachers believe in alphabetical seating. In French, Algebra, and Honors English the real subject I am studying is the back of Randy Callahan's head.

Randy's thick, silky blond hair always shines. It is cut short but full in back, exposing a neck both graceful and powerful. In this light I can make out the faint, downy blond hairs that cover it, and a shudder runs through me.

He shifts around and catches me staring. "You're Coach Callaway's daughter, aren't you?"

"Yeah." My face is hot. "I'm Susan. Is that your team out there?" I wave toward the field. "Baseball, I mean?"

"Nah. Football's my game." Randy leans against the trailer wall, eyes half shut in the sun. "Your dad's a great coach. A great guy."

I let out a breath. "Thanks. He is."

We are quiet together, and I am feeling much calmer.

"You're not in this class, are you?" I ask him finally. Randy opens his eyes, doesn't say anything. "I mean, if you have a note for Mr. Duffy or something, I could—"

He gestures past me. "Here they come."

I turn just as Mr. Duffy calls, "Hi, kids!" He trundles along the narrow path between the tennis courts and the series of trailers that lead to Voc Ed.

Three Wayne High students trail after him, single file at widely spaced intervals: Tracee Ellison, Kale Krasner, and Amber Hawkins.

"Oh my God," I whisper, looking harder. But it is still Tracee Ellison. Kale Krasner. Amber Hawkins.

"Twelve meetings," Randy says. I turn back and see that same grin. "Now till June. We can do it."

I feel something stirring. It is happiness. It is hope. If Randy never talks to me again, he has talked to me now, and I will remember this.

"Thanks." I duck my head. Randy has already stood to greet Tracee, his true peer. It's okay, though.

We had a moment.

4
Warm-up

Mr. Duffy says, "Circle up!" and after a blank pause Randy heads for a stack of chairs against the far wall. One by one the others follow. I am last.

Kale pauses as our paths intersect. Holding his chair in front of him like a locomotive, he leans in to deliver a soft pig snort in my ear. I flinch, hoping no one else has heard. But Amber has, and she grins at Kale. Tracee regards the three of us with an expression that could strip paint. I don't know which of us has earned her disgust, but I look away fast, glancing up at the clock. Three-thirty-nine. Great.

Amber muscles past Tracee and swings a chair out from the wall, nearly hitting her.

"Hey!" Tracee jumps back, a hand to her chest. "Watch it!"

"Watch this, bitch," Amber says, and walks off with a swagger.

Tracee looks to me as an outrage outlet. I give her a blank face back.

Muttering something under her breath, Tracee turns and lifts a chair from the stack. A silver bracelet slides down her slim arm, and I make out the letters engraved on it: WWJD. I wonder what they mean, decide I don't care.

I am last to the rough circle they have formed. I set my chair in the gap between Tracee and Amber.

"You're all here," Mr. Duffy says. He has added a pair of half glasses to his pumpkin face, and he peers over them to give a circlewide grin. "Callahan, Callaway, Ellison, Hawkins, Krasner . . ." He pauses. "No. One more to come."

"Mr. Duffy, question," Randy says. "Are we going to be out of here by four-thirty? I have to be somewhere later."

Tracee shifts. "Me too. My boyfriend's out there waiting for me."

"The sessions will last an hour," Mr. Duffy says. "And this one hasn't started yet. Let's give our sixth member a chance to arrive. First meeting; he may have gotten lost."

I see rather than hear Randy sigh. Tracee is pouting. I'm wondering why they could possibly be in this room.

Randy is an unlikely candidate for expulsion; Tracee as kick-out material is plain ridiculous. Tracee is a junior, and a cheerleader. She is also shorthand around Wayne High for a hot girl. "You know Heather?" I might hear my brother say to Scott. "She's no Tracee Ellison, but not bad."

I am conscious suddenly of sitting next to the prettiest girl in the room, maybe in the school. I am sure someone will point it out, the contrast between us. I try to make myself smaller, my legs pressed together, hands clasped, head down. Something catches my eye. Kale, directly across, is staring at me. His cheeks are puffed out like a blowfish, and when our eyes meet, he half raises his arms in a kind of bodybuilder's gesture, tapping his knuckles together in front of his chest.

I shift my gaze back to my lap, but not before the message is received.

Hey, did you know you're fat?

Weight-check time. I am not the fattest in the room. Mr. Duffy has me beat by at least sixty pounds. Maybe more. Randy's ahead of me too, by a good twenty pounds. Of course, Randy is about six feet tall, whereas I am five foot three, but still.

Kale's small. Small and thin. Stacked-heel cowboy boots and a black blocked cowboy hat can only do so much. Doesn't matter. He has me down.

The girls:

Tracee, forget about it. She is short, like me, but somehow manages to look long-legged in petite jeans. If she breaks 100, it's not by much.

Amber Hawkins probably breaks 150, but like Randy, she is tall; maybe five foot nine. She is attractive in a tough way, her face heavily made up, thick black hair in a fall straight down her back.

I have heard girls laughing about Amber Hawkins. Laughing quietly.

Amber's a slut.

Amber's a skank.

Amber can kick your ass.

I remember the day last fall when I saw Kale teasing a stray dog at lunch, coaxing it close with a hot-dog bun, hitting it with a stick whenever the little mutt was close enough to grab at the bread. I had hurried past, hating him, relieved that for the moment he wasn't targeting me. One girl from his crowd had grabbed the stick away. Amber. I see her again kneeling by the tangled mop of a dog, feeding it out of her hand. I remember how warm I had felt toward her that day. I remember how she smiled moments ago when Kale made fun of me.

"This guy we're waiting for," Kale bursts out. "What if he wasn't in school today or something? We just going to sit here?"

Someone knocks at the door. Everyone turns to stare.

"Come in," Mr. Duffy calls.

The knob turns slowly and I am eager for the distraction, one more distraction from me.

A boy steps into the room. His step is tentative, his face red. I draw in a breath. It is Brendan Slater, Brendan-from-the-library. Of course if I am here, he would be too.

But the two of us in the same room. Too much.

Target practice. Line 'em up!

I can't help but look at Kale. His eyes are wide, focused on Brendan.

"You have got to be kidding," he says. "Come on, Mr. Duffy! That's in here with us?"

"Brendan, welcome!" Mr. Duffy's voice is hearty. "Grab a chair and have a seat here by Susan."

A shudder passes through me, and not the kind I felt with Randy.

Thanks, Mr. Duffy. Put the losers together, is that it? The no-hopers, the victims, the . . .

Brendan's scent is pleasant, light and woodsy. Underneath I catch a faint odor of sweat. He sits, hands curled against his thighs—curled, but I see them shaking. Kale has his eyes on both of us.

5
WHAT I SAW

THE LEFT HEADLIGHT IS BUSTED, THE DRIVER'S SIDE *mirror is on the pavement, and Brendan Slater is shaking a can of spray paint. The click-click is the only sound in the parking lot, empty of humans but for us. I can't swallow, my heart too high, but I am not scared.*

He senses my presence and turns in slow motion, clutching the can, suspended, waiting. Expressionless, he takes me in. I look back boldly, wanting to show him whatever he needs to see.

"Don't stop," I tell him.

Brendan turns back to the truck and extends his arm. A hiss, a chemical smell, and the first spray of black paint washes across Kale Krasner's windshield.

6
First Session

"Now that we're all here, let's get started," Mr. Duffy says.

"I'm sorry I was late." Brendan's voice is quiet. "I didn't know where this place was. I had to ask a janitor."

"You made everyone else late too," Kale shoots at him. "We're all going to have to sit here longer because of you."

"As I said, let's get started." Mr. Duffy waits until Kale moves off Brendan. "Each of you did something that normally would have gotten you tossed from Wayne High. Instead you're here, in this trailer, and together we're going to make the time count."

"So we all messed up," Kale says, heels dug into the cheap carpet. "What are we supposed to do about it here?"

"We're going to talk," Mr. Duffy says. "Just talk."

"Do we have to say what we did?" Amber asks.

"That's your call," Mr. Duffy says. "My objective is for you to come to know one another."

"We go to school together," Tracee says. "We already know each other."

"You know them by sight. That isn't the same as knowing them."

"Mmm." Tracee stifles a yawn.

"You'll find me easygoing," Mr. Duffy says, "but I have one rule that can't be broken: What we talk about here doesn't leave the room."

"What if we don't talk at all, Duffy?" Amber's eyes are narrowed. "You going to make us?"

After a short silence, Mr. Duffy laughs. "I can't force anyone to talk, but group attendance is mandatory, and you do have to listen to what the others say."

"I ain't talking," Amber mumbles. She slumps in her chair, picking at a cuticle. "Nobody's business what I did."

Kale is her opposite, his black olive eyes scanning the rest of us, lingering on Brendan, lingering on me.

"Susan, you're a very quiet girl," Mr. Duffy says. "I doubt if anyone in this group knows much about you."

Or cares. Move on, move on.

"Tell us a little about yourself."

I give him silence.

"If you prefer, I can have the group ask you specific questions."

I catch the gleam in Kale's eyes when he registers what Mr. Duffy has said.

Why are you so fat—how much do you weigh—hey, do you know you're ugly?

"I'm Susan Callaway," I say as Kale opens his mouth. "My dad coaches football and teaches PE and he's the athletic director here too. We moved to Wayne when I was seven. In two years when I get my diploma, I'm out of here."

"To where?" Mr. Duffy asks.

"I don't know. Some college, I guess."

"To study . . . ?"

"Pizza making!" Kale shouts, and everyone jumps. I realize how quiet we have all been.

"To study what, Susan?" Mr. Duffy never looks at Kale.

My heart is thumping. "English. Maybe film," I tag on in a whisper.

"Very good. Tracee, let's hear about you. Where do you see yourself in five years?"

She crosses her legs and tucks some hair behind her ear. "In five years I'll be a senior at Stanford, getting ready for law school."

"Politics in your future?" Mr. Duffy raises an eyebrow.

Tracee's return look is steely. "Yes."

I look at her. Tracee has no doubt, no hesitation. I don't think about the future. No one does at my house. We live season to season. The faces change on Dad's teams, but his intensity is the same. Off-season he is preparing for on.

Randy is talking. My head clears, and I listen.

"Susan's dad is my football coach," he says, "and I do pretty well in school. I have a brother—he's older than me. Mr. Duffy, is that what you wanted?"

"That'll do. Kale, let's hear from you."

Kale stares at Mr. Duffy. "Like what?"

"Something about yourself. Nothing fancy."

"Nothing to say." Kale glances around, popping his knuckles in sharp succession. I wince; next to me Brendan sighs. "Name's Kale Krasner. Born and raised in this county. I love my truck."

My arms are gooseflesh as I study the rug. Inside I am laughing.

"Amber?" Mr. Duffy says. "About you . . . ?"

"Amber Hawkins—that's all you need to know."

Mr. Duffy hesitates. "Fine. And it's Brendan Slater who's just joined us. Brendan, I'm going to throw a quote at you, and I want your reaction."

Brendan shifts. "Yeah. Okay."

"No justice, no peace." Mr. Duffy waits. The pause is so long I glance over at Brendan. In profile his face is masklike, too still to be real.

"All right," Mr. Duffy says, his voice gentle. "Anyone else? No justice, no peace. What does it mean?"

"I've heard of it," Tracee says. "That quote. It's from the sixties. Some guy named Malcolm X said it. It was about black people getting their rights."

"I remember that," Amber says slowly.

"You remember it?" Tracee is smiling at her.

"Yeah." Amber sits up. "From U.S. History. I was in that class too."

"What does the quote mean to you, Amber?" Mr. Duffy asks.

"I think that Malcolm guy meant if someone does something to you, you get them back. Otherwise you can't rest. No peace."

"Amber's right," Kale says. "You don't let nobody get away with nothing."

Doesn't that mean everyone gets away with everything?

I think the words, don't say them.

"That's not exactly what Malcolm meant." Tracee is hesitant. "I think he meant it in, well, a more peaceful way."

"No, it's like in football, if you're the better team, and you know it, you have to win," Randy says. "You can't rest unless you do."

Tracee rolls her eyes. "Everything's football with you guys."

Randy laughs. "Tell it to Justin."

"Justice." Brendan spits the word out. "The only justice is the kind you make. And the only peace is when everything stops. Someone killed Malcolm X, didn't they? Maybe that was his peace."

Silence, then Kale laughs. "What are you talking about, Slater? Making justice? Shit, you couldn't make a mud pie."

Brendan folds his arms across his chest. I watch his expression fade to blank.

"Yes, Brendan, someone killed Malcolm X," Mr. Duffy says. "But the people who believed in his cause kept on fighting. They kept fighting for their idea of justice."

"Is this about affirmative action?" Kale's face is crinkled like he smells something bad.

"Yeah, Kale," Brendan says in a monotone. "It's all about affirmative action."

———

I AM FIRST OUT OF THE TRAILER. I HURRY THROUGH the tennis court alley on my way to the student parking lot beyond and the quarter-mile walk to my house.

"Hey!" someone calls loudly from behind me, just as I reach

the lot. I don't recognize the voice and wouldn't stop if I did. Shouts directed my way are never good.

"Susan! Susan Callaway!" I know who it is now, and a glance back confirms it: Brendan Slater is chasing after me.

I release the breath I have been holding and wonder what to do. I look again but Brendan is alone. I slow, stop, and wait for him at the edge of the lot.

He is panting when he reaches me. "Susan, I want to talk to you."

I shrug, shy with him, scared despite myself. "I have to get home."

He nods. "Yeah, I'm heading downtown myself. Let's walk a little, at least." When I hesitate, Brendan shakes his head. "Don't worry. Kale's still in there talking to Mr. Duffy. I think he's trying to get out of the group."

Feeling itchy, I give a tight nod. Really, who asked him?

"My mom works downtown," he says as we start through the lot. "I'm supposed to meet her at her office at five."

"Oh, you . . . walk to school?" I say, glancing over at him, The Day of the Truck flashing through my mind. "From downtown?"

"No, Mom drops me off in the morning on her way to work. She's usually running late. I have all these tardies. . . ." Brendan trails off. "Susan, why are you in Duffy's class?"

I stare at him. No answer I can give would make any sense.

"It's my thing, the truck," he says urgently. "I told them you had nothing to do with it."

I remember that day two weeks ago. Right here, in this parking lot. The campus cop, Brendan, and me.

"You told them the fat girl, the one with the long brown hair, she didn't do it? That it was you, all you?"

Brendan is surprised by my smile, I can tell. "Something like that. What did you tell them?"

"I didn't say anything. No matter what they said to me. The campus cop, the principal, nothing. It was so great. They talked and talked and told me what a bad girl I was. I watched their mouths move like I had the mute button on. My dad's treating me like I'm strapped with dynamite."

We are matching grins. I notice we stand only yards from Kale's truck. It's fixed—beautiful, shining, cherry red. I nod toward it.

"You think he knows who trashed his truck?"

"No way," Brendan says. "He would have done something about it by now."

"What if he finds out?" I ask. "Aren't you scared?"

Brendan regards me. "Aren't you?"

I look away from him. "You must have hated Kale to do what you did. I hate him too. Worse than anything."

"Kale Krasner is nothing much." Brendan's voice is soft, and suddenly the littered asphalt parking lot disappears and we could be anywhere. "There's a million Kale Krasners no matter what you do."

I shift my books from one side to the other, push my hair out of my eyes, my fingers sticking in the tangle. It occurs to me how I must look, and he is standing there, watching me.

"Let's get out of here, okay?"

Brendan nods, and soon we are standing at the intersection of

School Street and Snell Street. I point right, opposite downtown Wayne.

"I live that way, so . . . see you in Mr. Duffy's class, I guess."

"Susan." He is staring at me. "It's not right, you taking the blame. You shouldn't be in that class. I feel responsible."

"Don't." My voice is sharp. "Don't." Softer this time. "I wish I had helped you that day."

We watch each other. I look away first.

"Anyway. I have to get home. Kale will be along any second."

"We have a right to stand here." Brendan sounds like he doesn't believe it himself.

"It's not just Kale." I glance at him. "Anyone could come by."

"And see you with me." Brendan's unfocused look reminds me of my father's.

"It's not that," I tell him, even though it is. "I'm afraid for myself."

"Afraid of what?"

I give him a look, wondering if he is kidding.

"Because you're a little heavy, you mean? People get on you for that?"

"A little," I say, biting off the words.

Brendan steps back. "I'm sorry. I don't mean to hurt your feelings."

"You're not." The words are automatic. Then I realize I mean them.

Brendan shifts his backpack. "I understand. I won't bother you anymore."

Now that he is ready to leave, it feels like a loss, not a relief.

"You walk to town," I say. "And people leave you alone?"

"No." Brendan takes a deep breath. "They don't leave me alone. I walk to town anyway."

I clutch my books tighter. "I'm not brave like you. I can barely take what happens at school. I won't go looking for it afterward."

"They win that way, Susan. You sit at home and they rule the streets."

Neither of us has to define who "they" are. "Okay, they win. But they win by forfeit. I don't have to stand there while they kick me to death."

Brendan looks like he wants to say something more, something important. I am blank, waiting, exhausted by the day.

Someone lays rubber out of the student lot. I cringe instinctively as a red pickup runs the stop sign and slides around the corner. As he passes us, Kale Krasner screams, "FREAKSSS!" out the passenger side window, holding the note so long I can still hear it after he has accelerated out of sight over the hill.

7
REPRIEVE

BENNY IS WAITING FOR ME WHEN I GET HOME. I SEE him standing on the window seat, his mouth opening in a muted meow when our eyes meet.

I sigh as I turn the key, feeling the tension releasing from my shoulders. As I step inside, I am already lighter.

In the kitchen, I set my books on the table, noting Tom's schoolbooks there already. He's been and gone. No sign of Dad either. My frozen lasagna–stained plate from lunch is soaking in the sink where I left it. I give the plate a quick rinse and stick it in the dishwasher.

Benny's purr accelerates as I reach down to him. He snuggles into me, ducking his head against my neck. I hug him like a baby and stroke his thick fur.

I set Benny down and rattle out some food for him. Benny's bowl is only half empty, but I like to keep it filled. His water has a dust clot floating on it, so I change it, letting the faucet run a few moments. He leaps to the counter and settles next to the sink, watching me, watching the water. I look again for Dad. He and Benny coexist, but it's easiest when Dad can forget he's around.

Benny fed and watered, I'm starving. I grab a can of Campbell's cream of celery soup out of the cupboard and have it boiling on the stove within minutes. I've already arranged a handful of saltines in a big bowl, and I dump the soup on top, peppering it well. I open the fridge and grab a Mountain Dew out of the twelve-pack. Soda tucked under my arm, soup bowl secured, I click my tongue twice. Benny looks up from his Purina with, I swear, a smile on his face. He leads the way up to my room. Inside I set my soup bowl on my desk, pop the Dew, and take a long swig. In satisfaction, in relief, I shut the door behind me and sit down to dinner.

The ringing phone brings me out of my nap. The room is dark; I see by my VCR clock it is after 8 P.M. I stretch, pleasantly exhausted, and decide to let the answering machine pick up. It's Dad, probably, staying over somewhere.

Whoever it is hangs up as the message comes on. The phone is in Dad's room, but I can hear the start of the message, Dad's voice terse and businesslike. I close my eyes again, but Benny jumps down from the bed and begins his "let me out" cry. As I get up, the phone begins to ring again. Tom maybe, calling in?

I get to the phone on the fourth ring, just before the machine kicks in.

"Hey, hello, is this Susan?"

The voice is youngish, male.

"Yes. This is Susan. Who's this?" I wish I had taken the time to turn lights on. I sit on Dad's unmade bed, chilled, clutching the phone, my fingers poised to disconnect.

33

"I have this friend at Wayne High, and he said you might like to go out sometime."

I wait, expecting to hear laughter in the background. I don't hear anything but traffic noise. He is at a pay phone, or on a cell phone somewhere.

"Susan, you still there? Yeah, my friend said—"

"Who's your friend?" I take a deep breath, hold the phone to the bed a moment to exhale. When I pick up, the guy is talking.

". . . didn't want his name mentioned. He says he's a real good friend of yours, he likes you a lot, and I will too. He says you're a real cute girl."

"Tell me who he is, so I'll know . . ." *how worried I should be. If this is just a mean joke or something worse.*

"You sound cute over the phone," he says. "What are you wearing right now?"

Staring out the window to the house across the way, I press disconnect.

I don't cry. I'm not scared. I am numb. This is not the first call.

8
WHO GOES FIRST?

WEDNESDAY AGAIN, AND I DON'T WANT TO TALK
with anyone. I am outside Mr. Duffy's office at 3:30 instead of the
trailer.

At 3:35 he bursts through the door, overloaded with files.

I fall in step. "Mr. Duffy, can I help carry those?"

He glances at me with a slight frown. "Yes, Susan, all right."

Mr. Duffy leans my way and I pull two folders out from under
his forearm. I hesitate when I see they are cumulative files on
Tracee Ellison and Randy Callahan.

I put Randy's on top, smiling as I take in the wallet-size pictures
on the front cover stapled in progression from kindergarten to
sophomore year.

Mr. Duffy clears his throat. I look up, embarrassed, and he nods
in the direction of the trailer.

The campus is quiet; school has been out forty minutes. I am
glad. Whenever I walk with another fat person, I feel twice as big
and four times as self-conscious, as if each of us has a flashing
neon arrow over our heads pointing down.

"I didn't expect people like Randy and Tracee to be in the group, Mr. Duffy. Real people, you know."

Ugh. I bite the inside of my cheek, wishing I could take back the words.

"Don't you feel real, Susan?" He sounds distracted, peering into the middle distance as we round the corner to the stairway.

Everyone is at the trailer but Kale. Mr. Duffy tosses the room key to Randy, who helps Tracee down from her perch on the top rail. No one takes any notice of me. I focus on Randy's back as he disappears into the trailer.

"Hey," Brendan says in a low voice as I enter the room. He is standing just inside the door. I nod, unable to meet his eyes, Kale's tag echoing.

Tracee and Randy sit together, their bright yellow chairs touching, their blond hair intermingled as she speaks into his ear. Amber is across from them, arms folded.

"Guys, let's shift the seating around," Mr. Duffy says. "Susan, I want you next to me. Amber, by Susan. Then Tracee, Brendan, and Randy."

Amber doesn't move, but after a moment Randy does, then Tracee. Brendan and I go for chairs.

"The way you all returned to the places you had last week," Mr. Duffy says when we are in the circle he wants, "that was animal behavior. Tracee, tell us, why did you set your chair in exactly the same spot?"

She raises an eyebrow at him. "I don't get what you mean. You're not calling me an animal, I hope."

Animals are better than humans, much better.

I don't have the nerve to say it.

"No, Tracee, I'm only pointing out how territorial we are, just like animals. We have to have our place. Might not be the best place, but it's ours. In your classrooms, in the cafeteria, don't you all have a spot that is yours and no one else's?"

"Assigned seating, Mr. Duffy." Tracee smiles at him.

I know Randy's back but not his front, and since he is staring at the ceiling, I take the opportunity to stare at him. I notice the powerful muscles in his forearms, the confident way he has his legs stuck straight into the circle, not the way Kale would, to trip someone, but because he needs the legroom and is not afraid to take it. Next to him, Brendan's posture is hunched, feet drawn in and crossed under his chair.

"We want to be safe," Mr. Duffy is saying. "We want that same chair, that same spot, because it is safe."

"It isn't the chair," I hear myself saying. "It's that if something worked one time, you want things to happen that way again. You try to arrange them that way, re-create the situation the best you can. That's all."

Mr. Duffy nods as I twist my fingers. Tracee nods too.

"You're right," she says. "Susan, is that your name? You're smart."

Tracee sounds surprised, but my compliment meter registers a hit. A blush heats my face, and I am glad Kale is absent.

"Smart," Amber repeats. "So smart."

Definitely not a compliment, the way she says it.

37

"Susan's right," Mr. Duffy says. "We go toward what works, to whatever is least threatening. How welcoming are any of us to new ideas, to new people?"

Randy shifts his view from the ceiling to Mr. Duffy. "New people break in at Wayne High. It happens all the time. Justin Wright came in new last year, and Coach wound up starting him at quarterback."

Tracee clears her throat.

Randy grins. "And yeah, he's going out with Tracee too."

"Um." Amber holds up a hand. "Justin Wright is a stud athlete. Someone like him can always break in. What about a new kid like *him*?" She nods toward Brendan. I brace myself. "Or *her*?" Without looking, Amber wags her thumb at me.

"I think you're mean." Tracee's voice is controlled. "Leave them alone, why don't you?"

Amber glances over and taps her denimed knee against mine. "I didn't say anything she doesn't know. Right?"

Surprised by the tap, and the rough kindness in her voice, I nod once. I don't look at Brendan.

Mr. Duffy breaks the silence. "Let's talk leadership. What does it mean? Who has it? Who doesn't?"

Looked in a mirror lately, Mr. Duffy?

I hide a smile.

Randy plants his hands on his thighs, glances at the clock. "Coach Callaway is a great leader, that's for sure."

"Don Callaway is a successful coach," Mr. Duffy says. "Let's talk kids. Any leaders among you?"

Randy shrugs. "Justin?"

"Why Justin?" Mr. Duffy says immediately. "Simply because he has the talent to quarterback the Wayne High Wildcats? Or is there more to it than that?"

"Justin's sweet," Tracee says. "I always tell him he's too nice to be a QB."

I have never paid much attention to Dad's teams. But I hear him talking football, talking endlessly on the phone to his assistant coaches, to Tom during our Sunday dinners. I know the players' names at least.

"My dad says Justin is really good," I offer.

Tracee smiles her approval. Something compels me to add, "Dad said that Randy's good too, and that next year he might have a shot at quarterback." I nod toward Randy as though everyone in the room doesn't know I'm talking about Our Randy, Randy Callahan.

"Justin will be quarterback next year," Tracee says with a cold stare. "His senior year. He had a winning record, didn't he?"

"Hey, Trace." Randy shifts. "First I've heard of this. Forget it, huh?"

I clutch the underside of my chair. "Sorry."

Mr. Duffy clears his throat. "Leadership in sports is one thing. But what about real life?"

"Sports is real life," Randy says. "Teamwork, discipline, self-sacrifice—the world would be a better place if more people thought like athletes."

My world would be a better place if Dad thought less about athletes.

"I love sports," Tracee says. "But some of the guys party too much." She glances at Randy. "I'm sorry, it's wrong. We go to the parties, Justin and me, but the way people act—the way they drink, especially. It's disgusting. I mean, sports are supposed to be healthy."

Amber laughs suddenly, explosively. "Jocks are pigs. Get real."

"Not all jocks," Tracee says. "Not all the time."

Amber gives her the once-over and shrugs. She glances at her watch, which has Donald Duck on the face, I notice.

"Let's get to know each other a little better," Mr. Duffy says. "Partner interviews. Kale isn't here yet, so I'll pair up with Susan. Tracee and Amber, partner up; Randy and Brendan, you too."

"What are we supposed to do?" The distaste is clear in Tracee's voice.

"One person interviews the other," Mr. Duffy says. "For five minutes. Then you switch. After the interviews are done, you share what you've learned with the group. All right?"

No one answers him. Brendan looks petrified. Amber is shaking her head. The rest of us stare at Mr. Duffy.

"Talk to each other," he says. "Ask a few questions. Get interested! Five minutes each. Now . . . go!"

I turn my chair to face Mr. Duffy. "Should I start?"

"Sure, Susan. Ask me anything."

He is an adult, and a teacher, and I can't think of anything to ask that he would answer.

What did Randy do? Why is he in this group? What can I say to make him like me?

Mr. Duffy is waiting. Close in, I focus on his bad tooth, on his sweat-stained white button-down shirt, on his unevenly barbered red corkscrew curls.

How can you stand to look the way you do and work in a high school?

When his friends ask, Dad tells them I am going to be a teacher. That's what he says to relatives too, the few we still see. Aunt Dora and Uncle Paul. Dad's other sister, Cecile, who lives in New Mexico.

How can I be a teacher when I can barely stand to set foot in a school?

"Mr. Duffy," I say, "do you like working here? At Wayne High?"

"I love it." He looks surprised.

"I hope you don't mind me asking." I am red-faced as Mr. Duffy looks at me quizzically. "But I was wondering if you were overweight when you were in high school."

"I was," he says. "I've put on some over the years, but yes, I was heavy in high school."

"Wasn't that . . ." I hesitate. "Kind of hard?"

"I got involved." Mr. Duffy's voice is sharp. "I joined the chess club, the Franco-German Association; I became team manager for wrestling. I went where I was needed, and I made friends that way."

I'll bet they were laughing at you, the chess nerds, the wrestlers too. Does it bother you that they laugh even now?

"I'm not much of a joiner," I tell him.

In our quiet, I catch the murmur of other voices in the room: Tracee's careful, Randy's patient.

"Time for us to switch," Mr. Duffy says. "Now I'll interview you."

Five minutes later the circle is intact. My heart is thumping. I don't want to talk, and I don't want to listen to Mr. Duffy talk about me.

"Susan and I will go first," he announces. Of course. "Susan likes to read, she's a movie fan, and she loves animals, especially her cat, Benny."

Tracee leans around Amber. "I love cats too."

I nod, catching my breath.

"More about Susan. She's good at English, does okay in math, and wishes she knew more about the night sky."

"The night sky?" Randy says.

"Constellations and everything," I tell him. "In summer I go out sometimes and lean against my dad's car. I look up in the sky and just wonder."

Like anyone cares. Shut up, please. You are making a total fool of yourself.

But Randy is nodding like he understands.

"Okay, Susan," Mr. Duffy says. "Let's hear what you learned about me."

Nothing. I see nothing in my head but Mr. Duffy's anger at the questions I asked.

He was a freak too. He doesn't want to be reminded.

"Mr. Duffy liked school," I say. "He joined clubs. He made friends. He thinks . . . kids should be involved more. He loves working at Wayne High."

Mr. Duffy is grinning broadly. "She has it!" he says. "Susan, you're a good listener."

And you believe the lies. I bet you didn't when you knew you were a freak.

I give him a shy smile.

"Tracee, what did you learn about Amber?" Mr. Duffy asks.

Tracee glances at her notebook. "Amber's lived in this county her whole life. Her mom is a bus driver for the district. Amber's parents don't live together. Her dad is up in Sacramento and comes down to visit a couple of times a year."

"Amber? What about Tracee?"

"Tracee is going to be a lawyer and prosecute criminals. She has a sister who's eight. She wants to be a 'good example' to her." I can hear the quotes in Amber's voice. "She likes ice cream, so she runs ten miles a week so she won't get fat. Besides ice cream, her weakness is for dumb guys."

Silence. Then Brendan laughs. I haven't heard him laugh before, and I like the sound of it, even with the word *fat* pushing at me.

"Don't worry, Tracee." Randy is chuckling too. "Amber just confirmed what we already knew."

Tracee's laugh is forced. "I didn't say anything about dumb guys! I said that because I study all the time, sometimes it's fun to go out with people who are different from me."

"Whatever." Amber shrugs. "Next!"

I am so entertained I barely notice the metal stairs shaking outside. But then the sound registers, and when the door handle turns, I know it has to be Kale. I tremble back into myself.

It is Kale, and he pushes past Mr. Duffy and me to grab a chair. I duck as he swings back, passing the chair just over our heads, setting it down with a clunk between Tracee and Amber.

"You're a half hour late." Mr. Duffy's voice is pleasant but direct.

"My fuckin' truck wouldn't start." It is clear Kale is spring-loaded.

"That's too bad," Mr. Duffy says, "but it's four o'clock and we expected you at three-thirty. What does your truck have to do with that?"

Kale sighs. He is close enough for me to smell his bologna breath. "I take my truck off campus at lunch. Today it wouldn't start, and a guy said he'd look at it after school. I been out there waiting for him for an hour!" He shouts the last two words. My shoulders hunch, and I look down.

"I'm sorry about your truck," Mr. Duffy says. Kale expels another sigh. "I'll do what I can to help after the meeting."

"I need to call someone," Kale says. "We live fifteen miles out."

He stands. Mr. Duffy stands with him, blocking the path to the phone behind the teacher's desk.

"After our meeting," he says. "After the meeting, Kale."

Kale holds the stare a moment, then drops into his chair. "All right. What did I miss?"

"Partner interviews," Mr. Duffy says, retaking his chair. "We were just about to hear Randy tell us about Brendan."

Kale grins. "This I gotta hear."

"Brendan Slater," Randy says after a glance at Kale. "He was born in Danville, in the Bay Area. He moved to Wayne with his mom freshman year. He doesn't have a favorite class and doesn't like sports much, except he watches baseball on TV sometimes."

Kale snorts. "Baseball! Guy probably likes the tight pants."

"Get over it, why don't you?" Randy looks at the rest of us instead of Kale.

"Get over what?" Kale's stare at Randy is murderous.

"That's about all I have on Slater," Randy says. "Oh yeah, he says he wants to make movies one day."

Unlike Randy, Brendan took notes. His voice is without expression as he reads straight off the page. I don't listen. I watch Randy. He stood up for Brendan. A freak.

———

THIS TIME IT IS KALE WHO TRACKS ME DOWN AFTER class. I recognize the voice instantly.

"Hey, you! Susan? Yeah, Susan."

I stop for him. I have to. It is not possible for me to exist on this campus if I run from Kale Krasner.

Does he know about me and the truck? Does he think . . .

Kale stands in front of me, too close. I watch him unblinking even as I shift my books to my chest for protection.

Who's the guy, Kale? Who'd you get to make those calls?

"That stuff I told Duffy about my truck being broke. It's true."

"Yes?" I am tense, waiting. He's not acting mad, and places no special emphasis on the word *truck*.

"You live around here, don't you? We used to ride the same bus in elementary."

I remember that. I remember how you used to yell "Rollover" when I would step onto the bus. I remember the way my brother would ignore you when you made fun of me, or smile sometimes at the things you said. I remember some girls who were friendly to me at first stopped because of the way you treated me. They didn't want it to happen to them.

"We rode the same bus in elementary," I agree.

Kale bares his teeth, so fast I step back. But it is a smile, not a snarl.

"So you live close, right? The phone in Duffy's room wasn't working. You mind if I use the phone at your house? I need to get ahold of my brother."

I take him in, stunned, trying to keep my face blank.

In what universe would I do a favor for you?

"Hey, you know, I'm kind of in a hurry," Kale says, shifting feet. "Can we get going?"

Walk you to my house? Let you in my house? NO WAY!!!

"My dad's not home yet, probably," I say, hating the soft voice that emerges.

Kale lifts his arm and slams it to his side. "So what if he's not home? I need the phone, I'm not coming over to rape you."

I hear the anger in Kale's voice. His words register next. I can't look at him.

"Maybe one of the others has a cell phone," I say. "Tracee or Randy—"

"You kidding me?" he says, leaning in. "You want me to ask Randy Callahan for his cell phone?"

"No, I guess not," I whisper. "Maybe Mr. Duffy can give you a lift?"

Kale looks past me, back to the trailer. "The Fat Man said he'd help, so he has to. You're not going to do it, right?"

Glad he has said it, not me, I shake my head.

Kale leans back and cocks his fist. I cannot believe it is going to happen, but my body reacts in a major cringe. He swings forward and I feel the wind as his fist stops a hairsbreadth from my cheek. He keeps it there, cocked, and I smell the oil and gasoline on his hand. All at once I am going to be sick.

As I turn away, Kale gives a harsh tug to the curls tucked behind my ear. His greasy hand slides over my hair.

"Fat bitch," he says.

I LONG FOR MY MOM. SHE WOULD KNOW HOW TO TELL Dad about Kale. Tell him so he would care.

I don't cry.

9
How It Was

MOM WAS SICK SO LONG IT BECAME A SETTLED
thing. Every change so gradual it was only later that I saw. Only
later when I knew that what happened was inevitable.

She got the diagnosis the spring of my fourth-grade year. Mom
was a teacher's aide in my class that year, Mrs. Easton's fourth
grade at Wayne Elementary. That summer, she had an operation,
while Tom and I stayed with Aunt Cecile in New Mexico.

Dad wouldn't talk about the cancer; Mom said not to worry. We
didn't, I didn't, because it seemed like they weren't. Dad cared
about his teams then, but he loved Mom and he cared about us
too; you could see it.

Evenings Mom and Dad would walk the track at Wayne High;
Tom and I would run the bleachers or play Frisbee on the football
field. Mom would tease Dad about how he couldn't bear to step
an inch off the Wayne High campus, day or night. It was funny
then.

She was heavy, and I was plump; Dad and Tom were tall and
skinny. He didn't get on her about weight, not that I heard. Mom
would care and not care; salads some nights, pizza and takeout

chicken most weekends. Diets that went nowhere. Dad's arms steady around Mom as she tried, as she didn't try. Tom and I stood back and lived our lives, Tom lost in a pack of guys, me with my best friend, Anna, who understood me.

Mom returned to work that fall, but she was tired, so tired after school she would sleep on the couch for hours. She cut her days at Wayne Elementary to three, then two. The following summer, another operation. Chemotherapy then, and that year Dad didn't coach, just taught, so he was free to drive her to appointments.

My sixth-grade year, Mom started with Tom and me at Wayne Elementary, but by mid-September she had to take a leave. She was always on the couch after that, except at night, when we couldn't help but see the trouble she was having with the stairs.

They don't get along with your father, she would explain, when I asked why no one came, no one at all to visit. My relatives, she would say, they don't see him like I do.

I wondered how Dad's relatives saw him, because we hardly saw them either.

She began to talk less, but listened so well you hardly noticed. She talked enough to tell us how Dad was feeling, to tell him what we needed to keep going. From the living room couch she stayed at the center of our lives.

Sixth grade was when my body began to develop out of control. No one noticed at home; Tom was out mostly, lost with his friends, and I could not tell Mom and Dad that the teasing I had always faced at school now centered around my chest. I gained weight everywhere else too, moving from plump to fat in hardly a moment, it seemed to me. Aunt Cecile showed up uninvited one day and took me to the store for new bras her first afternoon in town. A few shirts too. She lectured Mom, and Dad came home to find Mom crying. That was the end of Aunt Cecile.

The living room became Mom's bedroom, officially. Tom and I never knew what we would find when we came home. Sometimes she wasn't there at all, in the hospital for an overnight, two days, three days. In February Tom brought home a nasty cold. We all got it, but it would not leave Mom, ripening into pneumonia. A week in the hospital then, and they found more problems.

In the hospital we held her hand and talked, and she smiled and listened to anyone who held her hand. She couldn't talk, but she could whisper, and the word she whispered was *Home*.

So Dad took her home.

10
WHAT HE DID

IT IS MARCH, SPRING VACATION, AND DAD IS SCREAM-
ing at us.

"Get out, get out, get out of the house!"

Tom is twelve and I am eleven and all we can do is leave. It is cold
outside, just past 8 A.M., and neither of us knows where to go. There
is no chance Tom will go to Scott's house or I will go to Anna's. We
don't like each other much, but we have to stay together.

Tom jerks his head so violently his hair flops across his forehead,
covering his eyes till he flips it back. "Axle Park," he says, voice thick
like there are tears behind it.

I trudge after him on stubby legs, my feet crunching on the frosted
ground. In the distance I hear an ambulance siren approaching.

"Tom!" I scream at him, I who never raise my voice.

He stops, his back to me. He is wearing only a sweatshirt and
jeans on this blue-sky, near-freezing day. Dad had shoved Mom's big
white sweater at me on my way out the door. Today I don't care
how fat the sweater makes me look.

I catch up to Tom, the sound of the ambulance ringing at me.

"Do you think it's going to our house?" Even as I ask I know how stupid the question is.

"Yes, I think it's going to our house," Tom says through gritted teeth. He catches at my sleeve. "Come on."

We leave the paved road to Axle Park and hurry through the brush for the shortcut through the woods. We can't see the road anymore, but I hear the ambulance rush by the spot where we stopped. We live close to Wayne Community Hospital—"a great advantage," one of Dad's teaching friends had told him. A friend who never came back with his wife, never brought any more hot meals over.

Tom is striding again, and I rush to keep up. I will not mention the ambulance; he doesn't want me to. The path is packed dirt between barren blackberry vines interwoven with poison oak. I dodge a frozen pile some dog left. Ahead of me another pile leaves its mark on Tom's shoe.

"Damn it!" he yells, so loudly I hold back my nervous laugh, so loudly I shiver and don't feel the sweater around me at all. The sound of the ambulance has stopped. I know they are at the house.

Tom is practically running now. I don't know where he is going; all I know is that I have to go there too. I break into a run, no one here to tease me about my form.

As we careen around the turns of the path, I hear a piercing yowl, and for an instant I think it is the ambulance heading back. So fast? But the cry cuts off, then starts again. A baby? No, a cat, or more likely, a kitten. I am eager to see it but heartsick too; stray cats live in the park and I am not to touch them, not to go near them, Dad has said.

Tom pulls up and I am able to stand by his side. Ahead of us I see *three boys coming down the path: Kale Krasner; his brother Darren, who is a grade ahead of Tom; and a boy I don't recognize, tall and skinny, maybe fourteen, in a red corduroy Salvation Army jacket.*

The sight of boys like these would normally send me in the opposite direction as quickly and quietly as I could manage. Today I look past them to the shoe box jumping around in Darren's hands. Kale is holding the box top shut, but a thin, gray-striped arm pushes out for an instant just enough to slash his thumb.

Kale pulls his hand back as Darren and the other boy laugh. Darren shakes the box hard, up and down, side to side. The kitten inside yowls and howls.

"Kill it!" Kale yells.

"Tom." My voice is soft and urgent.

"Quiet," he says, and I can hear that he is scared.

This can't happen. I can't let this happen.

The corduroy-jacket boy has seen us. He nudges Darren, who says "Hey" to Kale. Kale turns, a funny mix of defiance and innocence on his face. He sees us, and his expression changes to the nasty look I know.

"Hey, Tom," he says. He gives me the once-over and sucks the meat of his bleeding thumb.

"Let the cat go, why don't you?" Tom says. But he says it head down, in a rush, and hardly sounds like he cares.

"No. Now get out of here," Darren orders, giving the box a quick flip so the kitten is upside down. I whimper, and Tom starts walking toward them. I hold my breath, watching, but he skirts the three and continues on along the path. Far beyond him, I see cars pulling into the parking lot at Axle Park.

The boys are watching me. Corduroy looks bored, but Darren is grinning, and Kale meows, tiptoeing my way with claws bared.

"Tom!" I call, and look at the box. Darren holds it loosely now, and the kitten starts to cry again, pitiful squeaks. "Please don't hurt it," I say, a catch in my voice.

Tom is back, red-faced. "Come on," he says with a gesture. "Let's go."

"Please don't hurt me," Kale says in a high voice. "Don't hurt little me."

"Little?" Corduroy snorts. "She ain't little."

"What are you going to do to that kitten?" My voice trembles and inside my big white sweater I am shaking.

Darren looks at the other two and they all laugh. "We're going to throw it in the creek," he says. "Maybe hang it. We haven't decided yet."

I look at Tom. He avoids my eyes. "If you don't want the kitten, I'll take it," I say.

"We do want it, Petunia," Kale says. "We want to kill it."

"But I'll take it!" I step toward him, just a step, but my shaking lessens. "You don't have to—"

Corduroy runs up and gives me a push. "Shut up, bitch!" he yells, looking back at the Krasner brothers.

I stand still, shocked, my shoulder aching. Tom reaches out to shove him back, and Corduroy stumbles and falls.

"Leave her alone!" Tom says, and grabs my arm hard, pulling me away from the scene with a force double that of Corduroy's.

I stumble behind him, my arm hurting like it never has before.

Tom doesn't touch me, ever, and I move with him almost as much from surprise as force.

I hear Darren and Kale laughing at Corduroy and calling him a wuss, and then we are far enough away that their voices are a blur. We are outrunning them as we outran the ambulance. Only we didn't, and it isn't nearly good enough.

At the back entrance to Axle Park I plant my feet. Tom releases me. We are both breathing hard, our breath visible in the frosty air.

"Tom, we can't let them hurt that kitten."

He is still avoiding my eyes. "What do you want me to do? There are three of them. I tried. Forget it, Susie."

"Can you forget it? Really?"

He raises his head. Tom's face is a mix of red and white, his skin fairer than mine and quicker to show his emotions. I know he wants to mention our mother, and how dumb I am being over a stupid cat. I look around, anywhere, to escape his eyes.

A man and two boys are getting out of an SUV, the boys rushing around to the back to unload baseball equipment. I scan their faces. I don't recognize the dad. But the boy, one of the boys, he attends Wayne Elementary with me, in the other sixth-grade class. He is a cool kid, and I am not, but he can stand up to Kale. And his dad, maybe his dad will help.

I would never, ever, do this for myself. But to save the kitten, I can. I rush to the boy, Randy Callahan.

"Randy, hey, Randy!" He is staring at me. "You know that guy, that real jerky guy from school, Kale Krasner? He's back there." I gesture behind me to the woods. "He's going to kill this kitten. He has it in a box, and . . ."

Randy is looking over my head. I turn and see his dad, a big dark-haired man.

"Dad," Randy says hesitantly. "This girl . . ."

"What's your name, honey?" the man asks. He is staring at me.

I look down and notice I am wearing slipper socks, not shoes. And I remember I never combed my hair that morning. Mom's sweater is stained down the front with cranberry juice, and my jeans are ripped at the knees.

I decide that I don't care. I stand straighter and look at Randy. "Please help. Kale Krasner and his brother and his friend are going to kill a kitten in the woods right now. I'll take the kitten. I told them I would, but they won't give it to me. To you, they will."

No one moves. I see Tom in the distance, leaning against the baseball bleachers, his face now entirely red. I don't care about that either.

"Please," I say again, softly.

"Go on, son," the man urges. "Get her the kitten. I'll back you up if you need me."

Randy swallows, nods, and strides off toward the woods. His dad follows several paces behind. He calls over his shoulder, "Kevin, wait with the girl."

The boy standing next to me yells, "Okay, Dad!" in a thick voice that makes me wonder if he has a cold. I look at him closely, wondering what grade he is in. I realize he is retarded. His face is Randy's, but softer, his eyes smaller, mouth larger. He smiles at me.

"I'm Kevin," he says, welcome in his eyes, on his face.

"Hi, Kevin," I say, tears springing to my eyes for the first time that day.

When I see Randy and his dad at the park entrance, shoe box in Randy's hands, I let out a huge breath and smile over at Tom. He is staring at me, and not in a friendly way.

Randy looks grim as he hands me the silent, unmoving box.

"Thank you," I whisper. I set the box on the SUV's bumper and peek inside. The gray-and-brown-striped kitten is crouched, panting, but it is alive. It lifts its head to look at me and opens its mouth in an almost silent squeak. Enchanted, my heart beating fast, I gently touch its head, remembering Aunt Cecile's cats on her ranch.

"I love him. Thanks, Randy. Thank you so much."

He gives me an odd look and turns to his dad.

"You're Don Callaway's kids, aren't you?" the man says. "Son, come join us," he calls to Tom, who ambles over after a moment's hesitation. "I played softball with your dad last summer. Let me give you a ride home."

"Dad," Randy says, "I have to set up for batting practice. The guys will be here soon."

"Set up for practice then," Mr. Callahan says, his voice sharp. "And Kevin stays with you."

"Yes, sir," Randy mumbles.

Mr. Callahan doesn't drive us straight home. He stops at a mini-mart and buys cat food and doughnuts and milk. We eat in the car, sitting in the mini-mart parking lot, and I feed bits of doughnut soaked in milk to the kitten. Nobody talks, but by the time Mr.

Callahan starts the car, the kitten is curled in my lap, a steady purr rattling his body. I can't stop smiling, smoothing his whiskers on both sides.

At the house Mr. Callahan goes in first. We trail after, and Tom keeps going, straight upstairs. I hesitate, peeking into the living room. The special bed with raised slats is empty, and my dad and Randy's dad are standing next to it, talking quietly.

Dad sees me. His face is blank, dragged down of all expression. He glances at the kitten in my hands and nods once.

"All right, Susie," he says, voice breaking. He turns away, sobbing into Mr. Callahan's arms. I cradle the kitten the same way and tiptoe upstairs with him.

I hide in my room, Tom in his. Mom is gone. Dad never mentions her again.

11

Why Don't You Wear Nicer Clothes?

SPRING AT WAYNE HIGH SCHOOL IS A MATING DANCE. I noticed it as a freshman, how much of high school life is lived in sexual attraction. Now, as a sophomore, it hits me harder as I scurry along the edges.

Not you not you not you.

Girls I knew from Wayne Elementary, regular girls, not pretty, have bloomed. The skinny girls are slender now, small-breasted and narrow-hipped. Faces once plain are almost-pretty under makeup skillfully applied, and hair that hung long and straight flows, somehow, around their laughing faces. The dumb ones, the ridiculous ones, the ugly ones with good bodies, all of them are in the game.

I am not. I am determined not to care. I am short and fat and I am not going to deny it by aping the girls who can play. I wash my face, comb my hair, brush my teeth, and that is the extent of my grooming program. In the cold I hide my body in long, bulky sweaters. On rainy days I add an umbrella. For weather in-between I stick to a uniform of mock turtlenecks and baggy jeans. I won't get on the scale, but I suppose it is a victory of sorts that the jeans fit the same as last year.

On the day of our third meeting it is eighty-five degrees. Inside the Voc Ed trailer, the stale air barely cut by a laboring swamp cooler, it feels like ninety-five. Or 105. I push my drooping sleeves past my elbows, my hands clammy on the hot flesh of my forearms.

Like me, Tracee is wearing a turtleneck today, but the resemblance ends there. Tracee's is sleeveless red over slim-fitting white jeans. Her toenails are polished pink in delicate sandals. Next to her I am the Frog Prince.

Amber is less elegant in a shapeless green tank top, but her arms are on display too, powerful yet shapely.

Kale has on his usual outfit of T-shirt and jeans, but Brendan is dressed for the weather in long shorts and a light-colored polo shirt.

Randy is wearing shorts too, and his legs are sprawled wide. I note the curly blond hair on his legs, follow the trail past his shorts to his flat, well-muscled bare stomach, to the green cut-off football jersey stamped with his number, 15, past his bare arms folded across his chest right into his amused blue eyes.

I wrench away to focus on the black backpack Brendan has stowed between our chairs. Flooded with heat now inside as well as out, I am finding it hard to breathe.

Mr. Duffy claps his hands. "Today I want each of you to reveal something about yourself that no one knows. A fascinating fact you want to share."

"Lame," Amber mutters.

"And," Mr. Duffy says, his smile fixed, "I want you to think of a question for another group member, something you're dying to know."

Kale laughs. "How about nothing?"

You are nothing, Krasner. Dumbass bully. Hate you hate you hate you. Hate. You.

"What's your ambition, everyone?" Mr. Duffy is starting to sound desperate. "Tracee?"

"I said before, Mr. Duffy. Politics. Major politics."

"First woman president here," Randy says.

Tracee looks sideways at him but doesn't take the bait. She pushes her hair back and finger-combs it briskly. I notice her WWJD bracelet again.

"What does that mean?" I ask before I can think to be self-conscious.

Hair fluffed, even mussed for her, Tracee zeroes in. "You mean my bracelet? WWJD?"

"Susan, how can you not know that?" Brendan asks.

I look away from both of them. "Forget it, okay?"

"No, Susan, it's all right. Really. " When I look back, Tracee is smiling at me. "WWJD means 'What Would Jesus Do.' It's what I ask myself whenever I face a challenge. My mom and dad bought me this bracelet on my thirteenth birthday. I've worn it every day since then, and there's been times—"

"So why are you in here with us?" Amber cuts in.

"I was talking to Susan, not you." Tracee's voice is calm.

"Haven't you seen them, Susan?" Brendan says. "All the WWJD kids praying around the flagpole before school? Tracee, Justin, and all of them?"

61

I shake my head. I never come to school that way, by the main entrance.

"Brendan, you've seen us?" Tracee smiles at him.

"I've seen you," he agrees.

"They're okay," Randy says. "Those kids, praying and all that. It's different when you grow up with it every day."

"What do you mean?" I can't help but ask.

Randy looks at me. "My dad's a chaplain. A police chaplain. I thought you knew that."

———

MR. CALLAHAN CAME BACK A FEW TIMES. I WOULD PEEK out my bedroom window whenever I heard the knock. He was the only one who came.

Dad wouldn't answer the door. By August he was rarely home to answer it anyway. More and more he lived in his office at Wayne High. That was the year his teams started to play like madmen. Like they had nothing left to lose, and the Wayne Telegraph *took serious notice—other papers throughout the Central Valley too.*

The house belonged to me. Benny and me. Tom was always out. Anna moved away. There was nowhere for me to be but home.

Randy approached at school once, awkward, glancing around so much I could feel his shame at talking to me.

"Dad said to tell you if there's anything you need, you know, just call. If you want to come over sometime and talk to him or my mom, or if your dad does, or your brother . . ."

He was backing away by the time I could muster a response. "We're okay, thanks," I said, chin down, arms folded. Out of the corner of my eye I caught the relief on his face.

RANDY IS WAITING NOW.

"No, I didn't know he was a chaplain," I say, almost whispering.

Kale watches, his eyes reptilian. I shudder when I think of Benny in his hands.

"Are you interested in that profession, Randy?" Mr. Duffy asks.

Randy puts his hands out in a stop sign. "Not me. My dad would laugh if he heard you ask me that."

Furrowed brow. "Why is that?" The attention is off me.

"It's not for me, okay?" Mr. Duffy waits as Randy fidgets. "I'm just not that good."

Mr. Duffy and Amber speak simultaneously:

Mr. Duffy: "Define 'good.' "

Amber: "Is that what your girlfriend tells you?"

Randy ignores Mr. Duffy, stares at Amber. "I'm between girlfriends right now."

"Sounds good to me." Kale Krasner leering is not a pretty sight.

Mr. Duffy overrides the tension. "All right, then, Randy, let's hear something about you no one knows."

Randy expels a breath. "I'm not exactly a mystery guy." He raises his arms, and his shirt rides halfway up his chest. "This is me."

Amber catches me looking. "Just the way Susan likes you," she says.

UGH! I am happy the room is so hot my face is already red.

"Can I open the door, Mr. Duffy?" I say in a rush. "I don't think the cooler's working."

"Of course, Susan. Open the door," he says.

63

I'm at the door before he's finished speaking. I take a deep breath of outside air, and eighty-five degrees feels arctic compared with the hot box inside.

When I turn back, I notice Kale watching me. He tracks me to my chair.

"Look at her face!" he says. "Man, is she sweating."

"It's a hot day," Mr. Duffy says. "People sweat."

"What are you hot about, huh?" Kale leans forward. "Is it Callahan's ass or is it the weather?"

"Hey," Randy says, drawing out the word.

Kale gestures to me and looks around the circle. "What is she dressed for, anyway, the dyke olympics? Maybe if she didn't dress like that, she wouldn't be stinking up the place with her BO."

I do not stink. I don't. I know I don't.

I am statue-still. Waiting. Wondering if the others will laugh.

Mr. Duffy is pointing at Kale. "No personal attacks. Apologize to her, now!"

"You're scum, Krasner." Another drawl from Randy's direction, low, slow, floating. I feel it caress my cheek as it slides by.

After a moment Kale mumbles something I don't catch. Evidently it is enough, because now Mr. Duffy is asking Amber her secret ambition.

Tracee holds up a hand, and I catch a glimpse of silky-smooth armpit. "Wait. Mr. Duffy, can I . . . ? It was mean the way Kale said it, but I've been wanting to know too. Susan, why don't you wear nicer clothes?"

I will never be able to wear my uniform again. But I have nothing to replace it.

"I wouldn't ask if you were too poor or something," Tracee says. "But I know you're not. Your dad is Coach Callaway, right?"

UGLY UGLY UGLY blares in my brain.

"You wear the same clothes every day."

Not true. I have three different dark-colored mock turtlenecks I alternate with black jeans.

"Do you think we don't notice?"

We? A committee is formed to analyze Susan Callaway's clothes?

"Susan?" Tracee is sharp now. "Listen to me. Now that I know you from this class, I think you're nice and I think you're smart. Before when I saw you around campus, I thought you were retarded."

Randy sits up, then slouches back in his chair.

"You walk around school in those bummy clothes with this 'Everybody hates me' expression, and that is just a magnet to loser guys." Tracee nods in Kale's direction. "Are you really surprised when they go after you?"

My eyes burn. I know I am going to cry, the kind of uncontrollable crying nothing but time can stop. The kind I reserve for my room, Benny my only witness.

The moment passes. Kale is here. He does not deserve to see me cry. I am not that suicidal.

I take a deep breath and stare at Tracee. Return her stare.

She smiles uncertainly. "Are you all right?"

"How can she be all right after listening to your bullshit?" Amber says. "If Susan walked around smiling all day, they'd kill her worse, and you know it."

"That is not true." Tracee looks past me to Amber, as if I am not the one under discussion. "Shelly Martin is a good friend of mine, and she's heavy. She's into things, she's a cheerleader, and everyone loves her."

Kale laughs, his chair tilted against the wall, boots dangling. "Shelly the belly."

"Shelly Martin is supposed to be my fat role model?" I don't know where the words come from, but I like the sound of them. Cool. Hard. Whispered, though.

Brendan leans my way. "Speak up, Susan."

I clear my throat, grateful for the extra seconds he's bought me. "Shelly Martin is a joke," I say. "Don't you hear the guys laughing at her on game day, when you all walk around in those little outfits? They call her 'Cricket' because of the way her thighs rub together."

"It's not a perfect world." Tracee is shaking her head. "Shelly doesn't even hear that stuff."

Oh yes she does.

"Shelly's a mascot," I say. "She waits on you, laughs at your jokes, and holds your coats. Thanks, I'd rather be alone."

Randy is grinning. I can't help smiling too, a little, when he mimes applause.

"You're wrong," Tracee says. "Shelly is our friend. You're choosing to be alone, and I'm sorry, I think that's strange."

Strange stings.

"I bet you're not in any clubs or anything either. No activities, right?"

"Right." My voice is flat.

Tracee sighs. "How do you expect to get into college without activities? Good grades aren't enough."

I know she is right. The truth is, the only time I think about college is when I hear Dad bragging about my grades to his friends.

"I get it, Tracee," I tell her. "Okay? Thanks."

She leans forward. "You could look so much better. I'm not even talking about your weight. I'm talking about the way your hair is all over the place. It's so pretty, curly and thick. But half the time it looks like you don't comb it."

"Tracee, come on," Randy says quietly.

"You have a nice face. Pretty, even," she says. "But you don't wear makeup, not even lipstick. You combine that, the way you're always frowning, the clothes you wear, and you come across just so . . ." Tracee hesitates.

"She's saying you look like a dyke." Amber is smirking.

Kale lets his chair down with a clunk. "Like I said."

Tracee glares at both of them. "That isn't what I meant."

"You can't tell by looking if a person is gay." Brendan's voice is quiet but steady.

"You're the expert, Slater." Kale's voice is no longer playful. "Faggot."

"That's enough, Kale," Mr. Duffy says. "I want to see you after class."

"I have a question for him," Brendan says. "Something I've been dying to know."

"Careful, Brendan." Mr. Duffy shifts forward.

67

"Krasner," Brendan says, "do you like to make anonymous phone calls?"

———

AFTER CLASS TOM IS HOME, STRETCHED OUT ON THE couch watching a baseball game, with Benny stretched out on him, purring.

"Hey," I say, surprised to find him there.

"Hey," Tom says. He strokes Benny's head absently. "Dad called. He said he's bringing stuff home. Pizza or something."

My mouth waters. "Are you in trouble?" I set my books on the table in the hallway and join him in the living room. Benny sees me and jumps off Tom, running over to rub against my shins. I scoop him up, smiling.

Tom stays focused on the game. "Nah. Scott is. No visitors for a while, his mom said."

"Probably just trying to get rid of you." I am joking, but I see Tom's face tighten.

"Probably," he agrees, sitting up. "Where were you? You're always here after school."

I settle into the overstuffed chair, cross-legged, with Benny on my lap. "Nowhere. Just this thing."

Susie, you keep this quiet.

For a giddy moment I want to tell Tom about Mr. Duffy's group, and more particularly, about Kale's truck. I would have it for a moment, Tom's attention, his full attention. He'd laugh, maybe. He'd see I could do something.

"Bet I know what it is," Tom says. "Some counseling thing? For

68

being fat? I know, you have to sit there with Mr. Duffy or something."

Tom is laughing. Definitely not with me.

"I was just studying in the library," I say.

"Did you see your boyfriend there?"

This is a joke that never gets old, at least for Tom. He couldn't wait to tell Scott I thought a gay guy was cute, that I thought a gay guy liked me the way a "real" guy would. He had even tried to lay the joke off on Dad during a Denny's dinner.

You stay away from that kid, Tom. You and Susie both.

Brendan facing Kale. The shock on Kale's face.

Do you like to make anonymous phone calls?

The feel of Kale's grease on my hair.

"Yes, I saw Brendan," I say deliberately. "I like him. I like him a lot."

"Well, good for you," Tom says. "Just keep it to the library. That's the only place for that guy."

I shrug. He watches me a moment, then stands in a long stretch.

"Dad better bring home an extra-large. I could eat the whole thing myself."

So could I.

My brother never gains more weight than he should, no matter what he eats. He is skinny, still skinny, always skinny.

———

DAD TAKES UP RESIDENCE ON THE COUCH WITH A PLATE loaded with pepperoni pizza, his eyes on the same endless baseball game Tom was watching. Tom is upstairs now, with his computer.

"Dad." I keep my voice lowered anyway. "Did you want to talk about Mr. Duffy's group? How it's going, or anything?"

I watch ten seconds go by on the clock on the wall above Dad's head. I know better than to repeat myself.

"Susie, please. I'm watching the game." He half smiles, half frowns, turns back to the TV.

Benny is dancing at my feet, watching my plate. I'm three pieces in, and full enough to begin tearing the pepperoni rounds I've set aside into cat-size bits.

Dad looks over suddenly and catches Benny standing, paws dangling, as I drop a tiny piece of meat into his mouth.

"Aw, don't do that in here, come on, hon. Damn cat."

"Sorry." I want to grab his attention while I have it, but my tongue feels heavy. I remember what Tracee said about my clothes.

"Something up?" Dad is only half turned my way. His fingers tap the top of the battered green couch, settling around a can of Coors. "You need something?"

"I think I might need some clothes." I stand to lead Benny out of the room. "Do you think maybe this weekend we could go to the mall?"

"I'm on a conference this weekend," Dad says. "I've got something next week too. Didn't you check the schedule?"

It's true I haven't checked the big kitchen calendar where Dad blocks out his engagements. Haven't thought to check it lately.

"I've been wearing the same clothes too much," I tell him.

"This girl in Mr. Duffy's group mentioned it. I need to get something different."

"Have you looked upstairs?" From the side I see Dad swallow hard. "You might find some things there to tide you over."

Mom's stuff? I can't quite believe it.

"Sure," I tell him. "I'll check upstairs later."

This weekend. While you're gone.

"Susie," Dad says as I start to leave the room, "don't listen too hard to anything you hear in that group. Your job is to get through it. Nothing more."

"I know, Dad. Sorry. Hope you have a good trip."

He doesn't respond.

In the kitchen I grab two more pieces of pizza and a can of Mountain Dew to wash them down. A click-click of my tongue and Benny and I are set for the evening.

12
Weekend Interlude

Dad leaves for his conference early Saturday morning. I wake to the sound of the SUV's departing rumble. My first thought is of "new" clothes—clothes new to me, anyway.

I have made it through Thursday and Friday at school in my turtleneck/black jeans ensemble, Tracee's words constant in my head:

You wear the same clothes every day.

Do you think we don't notice?

But if I change, if I try, won't everyone notice more? Won't everyone laugh harder?

I resist the urge to return to sleep. I push the covers back and head for Mom and Dad's room.

My mother's special comb is on their dresser by the full-length mirror. I pull the comb through my hair, untangling the curls section by section. I look into the mirror and wonder. I see a girl with big brown eyes. Suspicious eyes. A round face. Hair that can frame her face or hide it. A fat body dressed in shapeless clothes. A rectangle—my at-home uniform is a big T-shirt over sweatpants.

Mom and Dad have a large closet, filled mostly with Mom's

stuff. Dad wears sweats to school—gold T-shirt, green athletic pants, the Wayne High colors. As athletic director, coach, and PE teacher, he spends most of his time in the gym complex.

I have wondered sometimes, especially since high school, if any of Mom's clothes might be right for me. I haven't dared to wonder out loud.

I am not as heavy as she was at her heaviest. Still, Mom had her dieting times. And the clothes from her illness.

With the operations and the treatments, Mom lost weight. She was excited, at first, at the chance to wear smaller clothes. But soon enough it didn't matter, and she lived in her own uniform: comfortable T-shirts and loose pants, almost like my at-home ensemble, except she wore leggings instead of sweats.

One by one I drape Mom's clothes across the bed, putting to one side the impossibles and the outfits too much like her.

I find three short-sleeved shirts, too patterned for me, but possibles. Then a few dark-colored T-shirts that might pass as real shirts. I throw in two pairs of blue jeans to add to my baggy black ones.

Mom's clothes smell musty, but then so does Dad's unmade bed. I take the clothes I have chosen down to the laundry room. I consider leaving the rest on the bed for Dad to find. I sit downstairs on the couch with Benny, channel hopping, nervous, my fingers tapping like Dad's against the couch.

No use. I hurry up the stairs and put the rejected clothes back where I found them. I wonder how Dad can stand to sleep in this room, where her presence is everywhere.

Their wedding portrait is to one side of the mirror. He is smiling, focused, clasping her hand. Her head is inclined toward his, her curls rich and glossy, falling forward over her shoulders.

She looks beautiful. She is fat.

———

QUIET WEEKEND. NO CALLS. TOM SPENDS MOST OF it on the couch. An endless round of HBO, MTV, and sports. We hardly speak, but I like having him around. Just him, not a gang, not even Scott. On Sunday afternoon I clear a space at the kitchen table and work downstairs, on French, on math, on biology. I am bored by the math and science, absorbed by the French. All of it is easy to me.

Dad is proud of my grades. I see it in his eyes, our moment of connection twice a year when I hand my report cards over.

Tom, a year ahead of me, does just enough to hold a C average for sports eligibility. What he doesn't say, what I never would, is that he is a C athlete too. On Dad's football team this season he warmed the bench as a backup wide receiver, in baseball he is a distant right fielder, and in basketball he plays only when the game is out of reach.

"Tom," I call, tucking the last of my French homework into the book, "need any help with your homework?"

No answer, but I hear the drone of race cars from the living room. I peek in but don't see any big feet poking over the edge of the couch.

I catch a glimpse of Tom outside the window. He is cutting the hedges back, the hedges along the walkway. He wields the clippers robotically, his arms pistoning, his back to me.

I knock on the window for Tom's attention. Nothing. I open the door, calling him. It is a warmish spring day, and the air smells good, the roses just coming on. We can work together on the yard, maybe, and face Tom's homework later.

He clicks away at a fast pace, ignoring me. The arms of the clippers rasp against each other, against the strong, thin branches of the rhododendron. It is a shuddery sound, the edge of nails on a chalkboard.

"Tom," I call again. "Are you deaf, or what?"

He turns fast, the clippers angled in front of him, the blades shiny with sap. It is then that I see what he has done. The section of hedge where Tom was cutting is barbered almost to the ground, a bald spot surrounded by overgrowth.

"You can't leave it like that," I say automatically.

He gives me a look of such dislike, I take two steps back, stumbling over the lip of the doorway.

"Who asked you?" he says. "You don't tell me what to do. You're not him. Or her."

I am used to indifference from my brother. Sometimes a casual friendliness. Not this.

"Sorry," I tell him, wincing when I hear myself stutter. "I just meant that Dad might get mad about the hedge."

Tom tosses the clippers down. "He won't notice."

"Maybe not," I say. "But I could help you with the yard. You know. Just for something to do. Or we could work on your homework."

"I have something to do," Tom says, heading for the doorway, giving me a look to move me out of his way. "And no, you can't help me with it," he adds on his way up the stairs.

I WANDER THE HOUSE, LOOKING FOR A DISTRACTION. I want to fix things; I want to find the right words to say to Tom. But he is like Dad. Silence is our only way through rough times.

I remember how angry Tom used to get as a little boy. Spitting, kicking fights at school; tantrums at Little League over his own mistakes. Mom would talk to him, soothe him, caress him with her words.

Dad would be silent. Silent. Silent. Nothingness. And Tom would come around. He would calm himself, in a way he wouldn't for Mom; would imitate Dad, a miniature of set face and tight mouth.

I never wanted Dad's disapproval. I watched Mom and she was gentle and easy with Dad, and he smiled at her. He talked with her, quietly, about Wayne High, mostly. It didn't matter what about. The subject was *I like you.*

And Mom's answer to him was *I like you back.*

I perch on the edge of the couch. An arm across my chest, an arm across my stomach. Pushing in. Cold. Disconnected. Wondering if Tom hates me. Wondering how mad Dad is, really, about the truck. Or if he cares.

———

A HALF HOUR GONE AND I AM STILL LOST. ALL IS silent upstairs. It doesn't seem right for me to pick up outside where Tom left off gardening. My homework is done. The house is in reasonable order. Standing at the hall bookcase, I read a paragraph of one of Mom's mystery novels, but the words scatter, meaningless. Watching TV is worse, and I pop it off, for the first time since Dad left, maybe, the background noise I had hardly noticed unbearable now.

I am standing at the picture window, looking at nothing, when the phone rings. I draw in a breath as though a stranger has tapped my shoulder. Tom gets the phone upstairs on the second ring.

I wait, believing, half hoping, that it is my caller. I wonder if Tom will tell him off. Tell him to leave this house alone. To leave me alone.

Or agree with the caller and laugh at me.

Fifteen minutes later my brother bolts down the stairs. I'm sitting in the hall chair near the foot of the stairs and he gives a start when he sees me. Tom has a piece of paper folded in his hand.

"Were you doing homework up there?" I blurt.

"Huh?" He looks at the paper and holds it against his side. "No, something else. I'm going out. If Dad gets in, tell him—"

"Who was on the phone?" I ask. My voice is hoarse.

"No one, just Scott," he says. "I'm going over there."

"He's not in trouble anymore?"

Tom gives me a look. "See you," he says. Then another look, a tilt of his head, toward outside. Toward the hedge. "That stuff before. Forget it, okay?"

"Okay," I tell him, too quickly.

He pauses at the doorway, half in, half out. "How do you stand it?" he asks. "Being in this house all the time? Being alone? I'd go crazy."

"So maybe I'm crazy," I say lightly, before the hurt can settle.

When he's gone, I say out loud, "You weren't alone, Tom. I was here."

77

13
IT'S NOT UP TO ME

SHOCKEROO: FOR OUR FOURTH MEETING MR. DUFFY
is on time, already in the trailer when the rest of us arrive.

"Last week was the ladies' turn," he says when we are seated.
"Today I want to hear from the guys."

"Short session," Kale says. "No guys in here but me and
Callahan."

At first I think he is excluding Brendan out of pure meanness.
Then I understand.

"Why do you try so hard, Krasner?" Randy says in the midst of
Brendan's silence.

I flinch. I have tried hard today. I have tried hard all week, al-
ternating Mom's shirts with the "new" blue jeans. And my hair is
under control. Held back, even, with one of Mom's imitation-
ivory hair clips.

"Brendan is a guy," I say. Quietly, but I say it. "Being nice
doesn't mean you're not a guy."

"I'm not nice," Brendan says flatly, just as Kale says, "Nice?
That what they're calling it these days?"

Tracee nudges me, leaning in. "You look good today, Susan."

I look at her, beautiful in a sleeveless brown vest over a beige tank top. It almost hurts to smile, but I do.

"Thanks," I whisper. "So do you."

"Kale." Mr. Duffy peers at him. "Do you remember what I said last week about personal attacks?"

Kale drops his chin. "Fine. Sorry. Okay?"

"Sorry about what?" Mr. Duffy asks.

"Mr. Duffy," Brendan says, "I'd rather have nothing than an apology from him."

Kale barks a laugh, his right boot tapping a tattoo on the floor. "I'll give you nothing," he says. "Just do your thing, all of you, the talk, and forget about me."

Brendan is watching Kale. When his glance shifts, our eyes meet. I try a smile but he looks away.

"It's Brendan in particular I want to hear from," Mr. Duffy says. "He's probably said the least of any of you."

"No, Mr. Duffy," Brendan says. "Sorry, but not me, not today."

"Don't let him scare you, Slater." Randy jerks his head in Kale's direction.

"Callahan, I'm telling you . . . ," Kale says, face half hidden under his brim.

"What did Slater mean last week about anonymous calls?" Amber's lips are quirked. "Kale, you been dirty-calling him?"

real cute girl, and I want to go out with you

"That's bullshit." Kale's voice is low. "Don't even joke like that." He glances at Mr. Duffy.

"Relax." Amber couldn't look more bored, surveying him. "I'm trying to stay awake."

"It's more than him that does it," Brendan says.

"That's messed up," Amber says. "I get joke calls sometimes from guys. Assholes."

me too

I have told no one about the calls. How can I tell Tom, or Dad, or anyone else the message, the joke:

you're a real cute girl

"The calls," Amber says. "They rag you because you're gay?"

Brendan shrugs. I watch him, fascinated.

"People are so cruel sometimes." Tracee gives Brendan a gentle smile.

"Maybe we should change the subject," I say, glancing at Kale.

"I don't know why people don't leave each other alone," Randy says, shifting. "Waste of time, people who go out of their way to be shits."

"Sitting back and watching," Amber says. "That's as bad as the ones who do it, I think."

"When I hear guys talking about Brendan, I stop them," Tracee says. "At parties and things. I tell them that just because Brendan is more civilized than most guys, that doesn't make him a homosexual."

"We shouldn't . . ." I clear my throat. "If Brendan doesn't want to talk about himself, I don't think we should."

"What if I am gay, Tracee?" Brendan says. He is almost smiling. "Is it okay then, when people say stuff about me?"

"Cruelty is always wrong," Tracee says. "But you're not really, you can't be . . ."

"Mr. Duffy, what we say stays in the room. Right?" Brendan

waits for his nod. "I want to talk about the petition. I want to ask Randy why he signs it."

Kale wakes up, tilting his hat back. "The petition," he says. "Best thing going at this school."

I look at Amber, who is watching the boys avidly. At Tracee, who is head down, hands tight in her lap.

"What's the petition?" I ask.

Randy rubs the back of his neck, my territory. "It's just this dumb thing that goes around every year. It doesn't mean anything."

Something taps at my memory. A Denny's dinner, Tom asking Dad about this thing he was supposed to sign, Dad putting him off, telling him to leave that stuff in the locker room.

"The petition?" My voice is quiet.

"Susan, just never mind," Tracee says. She puts her hand on my arm, and the shock of that silences me effectively.

"Brendan, what about the petition?" Mr. Duffy sounds formal, and I remember he is a school employee, not some kind of oversize kid.

Brendan is in control, somehow, of the room. "Sophomore year, everyone decided I was gay. I started hearing *faggot* everywhere I went. One day I showed up for PE and saw these papers tacked to the locker-room door. You know, like for a school election or something. I knew it had to be about me. Guys were laughing, and . . ." He looks down.

"First page said, 'We, the undersigned, refuse to share a locker room with Brendan Slater the Faggot.' Beneath that, all these names. Hundreds of guys. Way more than just my PE class."

I shiver, the hair on my forearms erect. Brendan's petition is the concrete realization of my own fears.

"What did you do?" I ask.

"I stood there," Brendan says. "I read the names. The guys were passing through to PE, and they kept swinging the door in my face.

"When the bell rang, I walked away. Out of the locker room. I don't know why, but I ended up at the library. I asked Ms. Henderson if she needed any help. She said yes. Since then, that's my PE. Helping in the library."

"Brendan," Mr. Duffy says, "did you complain to Ms. Henderson, did you talk to the administration, did you—?"

"No," Brendan says. "I loved her for taking me on, no questions. I was so fucking ashamed that day, that if someone had said the next wrong thing, I would have disappeared."

"Oh, don't talk that way," Tracee says.

Brendan glances at her. "I told my mom I needed a doctor's note out of PE. She got one for me, and that was that. Library city, all legal. The guys still went to the trouble this year to make up another petition, same words. They taped it to my locker. Just in case I didn't get the message the first time."

Something is wrong, beyond what Brendan has said. I look at Randy. "You don't sign the petition, do you? You couldn't."

He doesn't answer, just heaves a sigh.

"Randy's signed twice," Brendan says.

"Wait a minute." Randy looks from Brendan to me.

"He's not alone," Brendan says, smiling, a hurt smile. "Last year Randy was one of three hundred guys to sign. This year, one of two hundred and seventy-three."

"Jesus," Randy says, so softly I barely hear him.

"That's harassment," Mr. Duffy says. He points his clipboard at Brendan. "You need to tell the principal about this."

Brendan stares at our counselor. "You said this stuff stays in the room. You going to stick to that?"

Mr. Duffy looks away. "You know, it's a safe bet that a good number of the boys who signed that petition are gay themselves."

Kale is bolt-upright, following this like a tennis match. "Ain't the case."

"Look it up," Mr. Duffy says. "Ten percent, statistically, of any group."

Tracee raises her hand, then pulls it down. "Mr. Duffy, that ten percent figure isn't true. My pastor says homosexuals account for three percent or less of the population, and even that—"

"My uncle's gay," Randy says.

The room is hushed. Everyone turns to him. Kale's mouth is hanging open.

"The petition is ridiculous," Randy says. "I thought twice about signing it this year. Freshman year, the seniors were passing it around and I would have signed anything they put in front of me. This time I knew better, but I did it anyway."

"Tell us about your uncle," Amber says.

Randy tosses his hair back. "He's my mom's brother Hal. He comes up from Los Angeles every Christmas, and once during the summer."

"Does he come up alone?" Now Amber is snickering.

"No." Randy regards her coldly. "He lives with this guy named Carl. They've been together since before I was born."

"Aw, man, that is sick!" Kale practically screams the last word. No one looks at him.

"How do you handle it, Randy?" Tracee shakes her head. "I don't know what I'd do."

Randy shrugs. "Nothing to handle. Like I said, Uncle Hal and Carl come up twice a year, to visit and see the mountains and stuff. They stay in a bed-and-breakfast, not with us, but everyone knows they're gay. We just never talk about it."

"When did you figure it out?" Brendan asks. "That they were more than friends?"

Silence. Then Randy laughs, a deep, comfortable laugh that sends shivers through me. "I was around nine, and my best friend was Troy Garcia. Uncle Hal always sent a personalized Christmas card, you know, of him and Carl sitting out in their garden."

"I don't want to hear this," Kale warns.

"When the card came that year, I told my dad that when I grew up, me and Troy would live in a house together and send out Christmas cards with our picture on them."

Everyone is laughing except Kale. Randy glances around, smiling, red-faced.

"I didn't know what I was saying. My dad freaked out for a minute, then told me that Carl and Uncle Hal were a couple, kind of like him and Mom, and that Troy and I were friends who would probably go our separate ways when we grew up. I finally got what he was saying. I don't know which of us was more embarrassed."

"It sounds like you like him, your uncle," Brendan says.

Randy sits up. "I do like him. I'm sorry about the petition, Slater. I won't sign it next year."

"You going to tell them why?" Amber says, a challenge in her voice.

"Hey." A flash of anger. "I'm not going to sign. That has to be enough. This is Wayne High we're talking about."

"You'll sign," Kale says. "If you don't, guys'll wonder about you."

"Randy," I say, "you could get them to stop the petition. If you just explained. Guys would listen to you."

Randy points at me. "What we say here, stays here. Like Mr. Duffy said."

"But . . ." I look at him, strong, muscular, twice Kale's size. Towering over Brendan. Yet at this moment he is the smallest in the room.

"It's not up to me to save this guy's life." Randy jerks his head toward Brendan.

What you say here, stays here.

I have heard the saying before. I have lived it. Jock stuff. Callaway stuff.

Dad must have known about the petition. I wonder how much else I have missed along the edges.

14

CONFERENCE

ANOTHER WEEKEND, ANOTHER CONFERENCE. THIS TIME Dad returns with presents: identical XXXL-size T-shirts featuring the San Jose Sharks hockey team. He hands them across the table, one to Tom, one to me, as we settle in for dinner at Denny's.

Tom and I hold the shirts out and exchange a glance behind the fabric. Tom raises his eyebrows and I swallow a laugh.

As one, we lower the shirts, sober now. Dad is slouched in the booth, watching us.

"Thanks, Dad," I say. "This will make a great sleep shirt."

You do know I'm a girl, don't you? And yeah, I'm fat, but I'm not one of your tackles. You could fit TWO tackles in one of these shirts.

"Nice shirt, Dad, thanks," Tom says after a pause. In all Tom's sports viewing, in Dad's even, I can't remember one hockey game. Or any mention of hockey.

Dad's tucking into his salad. "I got them at this store called the Dugout," he says, munching. "I should take you two sometime. All the sports stuff you could ever want. Those two shirts were marked down. Ten bucks for the pair."

"They sell any baseball stuff there?" Tom asks. I give him a sideways frown.

Dad looks up. "Sure. That's the main product, San Francisco Giants stuff."

Tom loves baseball. Dad tolerates it, background music. Sports don't do a thing for me.

"Speaking of baseball," Dad says, "I've been talking to Coach Linder about your performance this year."

Tom straightens, the shirt balled in his lap. "It's preseason still."

Dad points his salad fork at Tom. "That doesn't matter. Practice sessions, real games, you give it your all."

I prepare to tune out, but I catch Tom's tension.

"Yes, Dad. I know."

"Coach Linder says you've been slacking in practices. Joking around instead of trying your ass off. It won't fly, son. A player like you, minimal talent, has to come strong with positive attitude. Fred would hate to cut you, but he'll do it if you make that choice for him. Got it?"

Tom hesitates. "Dad, I'm not the problem on that team. Eddy Rogers is the one who gets everyone going. Half the time I'm just standing there laughing at him."

"Step away from Rogers," Dad says. "He's talented enough to get away with crap behavior like that. You aren't."

Tom looks down, shaking his head.

"If Coach Linder is letting Rogers slide on his behavior, that's wrong," Dad says. "You know I don't operate that way. I benched that kid twice during the football season, times when we could have used him."

"We still went undefeated," Tom mumbles.

"Right." Dad nods. "That's my point. I could win without Rogers. Maybe your baseball coach can't. But he can get by without you."

"I think Tom understands," I say quietly. "The point, I mean." My brother sends me a sideways glare. "Dad's talking to me."

"Stay out of this, Susie," Dad says. "Tom, think of it this way. You were a valuable member of the football team this season without ever scoring a point. You did what I asked, and I didn't have to ask you twice. Make yourself useful like that to Coach Linder and you'll be around a long time."

Tom sits up for this. "You think so, Dad? I don't want to mess up in baseball. I want to, you know, play it in college, and—"

"College?" Dad laughs once, sharply. "Well, we can all dream." I wince, unable to look at Tom. Or Dad.

"Just don't embarrass me in front of the staff," Dad says. "Either of you."

I push wilted lettuce around on my plate. My stomach is gripped, absorbing the freeze of Dad's voice.

He is embarrassed by us. Both of us.

I think of Dad's coaching friends, the men I see him laughing with around school. His face is animated when he talks to them. He gestures, he smiles, he listens.

Those people are more important to you than we are, Dad. Why?

15
I Don't Care What Nobody Says

MOM'S "DIET" JEANS PINCH MY WAIST, BUT I LIKE
the way they look. My black baggy jeans drape almost like skirts;
in the blue jeans, you can see that I have legs.

I have tucked the black jeans away in the back of my closet,
folded neatly. I don't trust myself yet that I won't need them again.

I know how to diet—the mechanics, anyway. Eat less, exercise
more. Isn't that it? I am trying. I remember some of Mom's tricks
for almost painless dieting—low fat popcorn, elaborate salads—
and I buy that way on our weekly grocery runs. Dad doesn't comment on the different foods in our cart; he just pays for them. I am
more active around the house too, especially in the yard, picking
up some of the jobs we have all neglected since Mom died.

Another Wednesday morning I face the mirror in my parents'
room, combing my curls through, dreamy, half awake. The mirror
reflects movement behind me just before I hear a boy's voice.

"What's she doing?" the guy says. "Getting gorgeous?" He
laughs.

I turn to see Tom and his friend Scott in the doorway.

"Come on," Tom says, not looking at Scott, not looking at me. "My dad doesn't like us to bring people around."

I stare at Tom. "I thought you were gone," I tell him.

"I came back for my history book," he says, glancing over. "Scott, let's—"

"What have you been doing to yourself, Susan?" Scott says. "You look different."

I wait for Tom to say something. He is silent. I peer at Scott, but can't tell if he is putting me on. His smile looks genuine.

My lips curve into a slight answering smile. "I've been putting my hair back lately. That's all."

"Right," Scott says, nodding. "Your hair does look better." He gives me an up-and-down. "Now, when you going to lose that weight?"

Even though I am half anticipating the blow, it still hurts. "I don't know," I tell him, working to keep my voice even. "Someday, I guess."

"You wouldn't be that bad without it," Scott says. I still can't tell if he is joking.

I turn to the mirror, slowly, after they are gone. I am afraid to look again.

Mom is braiding my hair. We stand in front of the same mirror. The same picture is alongside us.

I watch her face. She is intent on my hair, serious.

"Do you think we look alike, Mom?" I ask.

She looks up, bobby pins in her mouth. Holding my hair in one hand, she squeezes my shoulder with the other, pulling me back for a moment in a quick hug.

I grin, trapped. My hair belongs to her. I can't move my head.
She releases me and quickly tucks in five bobby pins to hold my
curls in front. In back I feel tug, tug and the braid is done.
"Mom wasn't 'that bad,' " I say, to Scott, to Tom, to myself.

———

AMBER SLIDES IN NEXT TO ME AND DIRECT AS THAT,
busts me for trying.

"You're doing yourself up for her, aren't you?" Amber flicks her
hand at Tracee, who has just entered the trailer.

"Excuse me?" Tracee says, hands on her hips. Randy comes in
and gives her a gentle push forward.

"Please don't say anything," I tell Amber in a low voice.

She watches me, and I can't tell what she is thinking. Amber is
in full makeup today, eyelashes like spikes.

Mr. Duffy begins a spin about something, but I am not listening. I am noticing the way my thighs spread out over the yellow
chair, a little spillage on either side. I'm wondering, are chubby
legs better than the "does-she-have-legs" look?

"I have a topic, Mr. Duffy," Amber says, and my gut hits my
shoes.

She's going to talk about me, I know it.

Mr. Duffy leans forward. "Go ahead, Amber."

"Yeah," she says. "I just think it's sad how some people can get
other people to do what they want without giving a damn about
them."

Randy clears his throat. "Translation?"

Amber gestures to me. "Look at Susan."

"Do we have to?" Kale says.

Mr. Duffy frowns. "Amber, what is it you want us to see?"

"Guys never notice anything." Amber sighs. "Susan's all prettied up. Not for any of you. For Tracee."

I stare at my clenched hands. I wish for my uniform.

"You are really mean, Amber," Tracee says. "I think it's great Susan is trying to look better."

"She looked fine before." Brendan's voice is quiet.

"You're not being honest." Tracee's words are coated with syrup. "You know she looks much better this way."

O Gawd.

"You see?" Amber speaks into my ear but she is looking at Tracee. "This girl is not your friend."

I shudder at the feel of Amber's breath on my hair. Pull my shoulders in. Wish she would go away.

"Susan, I do consider you a friend," Tracee says. "Don't listen to her. I think you're really sweet."

Sweet. I make a face.

"What is it?" Brendan's voice penetrates.

"Nothing." I shrug. "I get that a lot. 'Sweet.' It's what people say when they're telling me I don't matter."

Tracee is frowning, her lips pursed. "I was trying to give you a compliment."

I hesitate on the edge of an apology.

"You just told Susan she used to look like hell," Amber says. "Maybe she doesn't want your compliment."

"Why don't you stop using Susan as your shield?" Tracee says. "You've been bitching at me since this thing began. What is your problem?"

"Watch it, girl." Amber is slouched, but her eyes are narrowed, her voice low but carrying. "You know how easy I could kick your ass?"

"Amber," Mr. Duffy says, "be careful. Remember why you're here. You don't get a third chance."

She looks at him. "I'm telling the truth."

"Mr. Duffy, I'm not afraid of her," Tracee says. "Amber, you want to jump me, go for it. You'd be picked off in a second and totally kicked out of school, and you know it. And I'll tell you now, my family would press charges."

Amber is breathing hard. "Real brave, Ellison."

"Girls who beat up girls are pathetic. Ask any guy. You can't win that way." Tracee sits back and crosses her legs, a hint of a smile as she surveys Amber.

A long minute ticks off the clock. The trailer is hot and close, the smell in the room chemical, like some kind of rug cleaner or maybe the shellacked plywood walls baking in the heat. Everyone, even Tracee, is sweating.

"I have a question, or an observation, or whatever," Randy says finally.

"Go ahead," Mr. Duffy says, relief clear in his voice.

"Susan," he begins, and my heart rate accelerates. "Tracee and Amber were throwing your name around. I was watching and you didn't even react. Why didn't you tell them to stop? I would have."

I take in his words. At first I think it is because it is Randy speaking to me that I cannot formulate an answer. But I know that isn't it.

He is still looking at me, his eyes patient, searching.

"So many people have said stuff about me for so long, it's wallpaper now," I say.

Come on, not true.

I stay focused on Randy. "I don't feel strong enough to stop anyone from doing anything to me."

"It sucks you feel that way," Randy says after a long pause.

I give him a quick smile. "Yeah, it does."

I smile inside. Someone understanding.

"Why do people get teased?" Mr. Duffy says. "Kale?"

Kale swings around at the mention of his name. "Why you asking me?"

"Anyone can speak," Mr. Duffy says smoothly. "Let's start with you."

"What, about them?" Kale flips his hand to me, to Brendan. "Everyone here knows, so what do you want me to say?"

"Your truth." Mr. Duffy's voice is quiet.

"Okay, her. She's fat," Kale says. "Guys think that's funny. If an ugly girl walks by a group of guys, it's got to happen."

"She's not ugly," Tracee says passionately.

"An ugly girl walks by," Kale says over her. "You're with your friends, you say something. Everyone laughs. BFD. Come on," he appeals to Randy, "you've never done that?"

"He doesn't need to," I say. "It's never guys like him."

I don't say more, but I dare to give Kale the once-over. A fast once-over.

Losers like you are the ones who do it. Loser!

"Same with me," Brendan says. "Then if I complain, people

say, 'Get over it.' 'Fight back.' How? That's what I want to know. What am I supposed to do, what can Susan do, to stop the shit?"

"I don't know," Randy says slowly. "That stuff isn't fair, that's for sure."

"Boo fucking hoo," Kale says. "Happens to everyone. No one in here would last a minute with my friends. They say worse stuff to me than you can imagine, and I don't care."

"Really, Kale?" Mr. Duffy asks. "What do they say?"

"I'm not going to say it here, and get in trouble." Kale leaks a nervous laugh. I almost join him. Points for Mr. Duffy.

"Why not?" Tracee asks. "You said it doesn't bother you."

"It don't bother me. It's friends messing with friends, so none of us cares."

"Don't they call you 'Little Dick'?" Amber's voice is thick with suppressed laughter.

"My middle name is Richard," he says, frowning. "The guys found out, so they call me that when they want to bust me. It don't mean nothing."

"Sure," Randy drawls. I look at him, delighted.

"We have established that words hurt," Mr. Duffy says as Kale's face reddens. "Can you see what we're getting at here?"

"What is this, everyone against me?"

"No, it isn't," Mr. Duffy says. "I want your point of view. I'm asking you to put yourself in the place of someone like Susan. Someone like Brendan."

"The porker or the fag? Those are my choices? No thanks." Kale's answer is automatic. It stings like a slap.

"You are so stupid," Tracee pronounces. "And my saying that

95

shouldn't bother you, because according to you, words don't hurt."

"No one said nothing about hurt." Kale's voice is raised. "I don't care what nobody says about me."

———

I WAIT OUTSIDE AFTERWARD. KALE BRUSHES PAST without a word. I am waiting for Brendan.

"Susan," he says almost formally as he comes down the steps.

"I liked the stuff you were saying in there," I blurt.

Brendan gives me a smile. "You got in a few shots yourself."

I am nervous. Embarrassed. I ask him anyway. "You want to go somewhere and talk?"

Brendan and I are quiet as Amber, then Tracee and Randy, leave the trailer.

"We could sit in the football bleachers," I say. "Unless you have to meet your mom or something."

"I have a few minutes," Brendan says, a question in his voice.

I gesture toward the field, and Brendan nods.

No one is in view when we emerge from the passageway between the trailers. In the whole expanse of the outdoor athletic complex the only creatures in sight are the glossy black starlings that haunt the field once the humans have disappeared for the day.

We slog through the damp grass, over the cinderblock-red track and up to the bleachers. I lead Brendan to the top row, my used-to-be favorite spot when I would come over with Tom. The sun is beating down and the bleachers are warm. I rest my back against a concrete ledge and stretch my legs. Brendan settles next to me.

"In the presence of mine enemies," he says.

"Here?" I am surprised. "You mean the jocks?"

He shakes his head. "Not exactly. The whole scene. Football. Rah rah. All that. No offense. I know your dad's a big part of it. Your brother too."

"You know Tom?" I say, catching something in Brendan's voice.

"Yeah. I know him."

"Tom can be a jerk," I say, picturing Tom with his gang o' guys.

"Don't worry about it," Brendan says. "You're not your brother."

"He's all right sometimes." I am not sure why I am defending Tom.

Brendan puts his hands out. Peace. "Why are we here, Susan? I thought you decided against it, hanging out with me."

I bounce my heels against the concrete. "Like I said, you could decide the same thing about me. You're not the only freak, you know."

"I know that," Brendan says. His voice is calm.

"I get phone calls too," I tell him.

"From Kale, you think?" Brendan doesn't sound surprised.

"It's not his voice. He might have a friend calling. I don't know."

Brendan laughs, a bitter laugh. "It's Kale calling me, for sure. Him and Jason Schrader. Maybe they think talking in high voices is the world's greatest disguise."

We are quiet. Wayne High is beautiful spread out before us.

"I still like movies a lot," I say, glancing at him. "Remember when we talked about movies in the library that time?"

"Sure," Brendan says. "I remember."

"Are you going to study film in college, like Randy said?"

"Yeah." Brendan rubs his chin against his shoulder. "I was so nervous having him interview me, I didn't even remember telling him that."

"Randy's a nice guy," I say brightly.

"Yeah. Nice." Brendan gives me a significant look.

I look away, blushing. "I love that class. I feel like I'm awake now. Every Wednesday. I love . . ."

Seeing Randy. Being with him. Listening to him.

"I love hearing everyone's story," I finish.

"It's working better than I thought," Brendan says. "When Mr. Duffy said Kale was going to be in the class, my mom about died, but I think it's good. I'm studying him like a bug."

"You knew he was going to be in Mr. Duffy's class?"

Brendan nods.

"You're not going to say anything to him, are you? About the truck?"

"I might. I haven't decided how to play it yet."

I smile at him, but I am worried. "Brendan, you can't do that."

"Why not? It's only high school."

His look is so fierce, centered on me.

"I'm scared of Kale," I tell him.

"I am too. I'm trying not to be."

"I'm trying too." My voice is uncertain.

His face relaxes into a smile. "Want to have lunch tomorrow?"

I stare at him, fast-forwarding, running a quick preview of Brendan and me sitting in my bedroom eating lunch.

"No, huh?" Brendan nods.

I want to touch his arm. Instead I nudge his knee with mine, Amber-style. "I'd like to have lunch with you. It's just that I go home to eat, and . . ."

"So don't go home," Brendan says. "I want to have lunch with you here, on campus."

It is a challenge. My stomach is twisting.

Make an excuse. Say you have a dentist appointment. Lie!

"On campus? Wow."

"We go here too. We have just as much right."

There is no Kale to break the deadlock, no way to go back. "Where do you want to meet?"

His smile breaks through unguarded. "The courtyard, twelve-thirty. Bring your lunch."

"I'll be there." I give him as much of a smile as I can muster.

In the presence of mine enemies.

16
LUNCH AT
WAYNE HIGH

"HEY, WAKE UP," RANDY SAYS, TAPPING MY DESK.

I look at him, startled. We are in Algebra. I have spaced my morning classes, spaced his presence, even.

Randy's backpack is loaded, ready to go, and he is sitting sideways in the desk in front of me.

"Class over?" I mumble.

He gives me an easy smile. "Yeah. It's lunchtime."

"She hasn't missed many of those," someone says from a few rows over. Melissa Carter, I think. I pretend not to hear her.

Randy looks away from me. He stands, shouldering the bag, and disappears from my focused vision.

His face stays with me as I gather my things: my notebook, text, and pencil. The book slips from my hand and thuds to the floor. Someone laughs, not Melissa, and I look around. The room is empty but for Mr. Haynes's pets, a half dozen or so, watching him diagram polynomial equations on the board.

Brendan is in the doorway, looking excited about something. Lunch? Our eyes meet and he says my name.

I hold on him for a moment, unable to speak or smile, watching, numb, as his face loses its animation.

Two girls on the edge of Mr. Haynes's circle have caught the action. They look at him, then me, then each other. They laugh together with the same sharp delight.

"Cute couple," one of them says, Melissa of the long blonde ponytail.

It is official. I weigh 800 pounds. No one but a freak like Brendan Slater would have anything to do with me. I duck for the textbook and stuff it into my backpack.

"Pathetic," the other one, Jamie Ross, pronounces.

Outside, I acknowledge Brendan with a weak smile. He looks away.

"Come on," he says. "I have this place I usually eat by the side of the library."

We skirt the courtyard, Lunch Central at Wayne High. The noise inside is shriek level, highlighting Brendan's silence. I notice how he doesn't hurry, how detached he looks.

The library wall is shaded by tall oaks, and the air is cool. Brendan nods toward a short set of concrete steps that lead to a side entrance I hadn't known about.

"Do you come out here for breaks?" I ask after we have settled on the steps. "I mean, when you're working in the library?"

He doesn't answer, just unpacks his lunch.

My face flushes. "I'm sorry for the way I acted in the classroom. People were laughing at me before you came in. Then those girls saw you, and they laughed at that because I'm always alone, and suddenly I have this guy waiting for me."

"And the guy waiting for you is Brendan Slater." He takes a bite of his sandwich.

No point in denying it. "Yeah, they laughed because it was you. They were laughing at both of us."

I fiddle with my lunch, the Baggie I have packed with a hard-boiled egg, celery and carrot sticks, and a handful of Wheat Thins. A little less than I would have at home. On-stage diet food.

"I hate people," I say quietly. Brendan glances over, still eating. "They made fun of me in front of Randy. He was talking to me before."

"He said hi to me outside the classroom." Brendan's voice is neutral. "He didn't have to do that."

I pop my Diet Coke. "Do you think it gets better than this? Life? High school?"

"I was going to quit last semester. Transfer out, hide out, run. Do whatever I had to so no one would bother me again. I don't feel that way now."

"Why not?" I am fascinated.

"My mom," Brendan says. "Duffy's class. You, even."

"Me?" I wonder if he is kidding. But I know that Brendan is not cruel.

"You understood. That day in the parking lot, with the truck. You didn't scream or tell me to stop. That moment, looking into your eyes, I felt less crazy."

"Maybe they're the crazy ones," I say after a pause.

"Tell me about your calls," he says.

I draw my knees in. "They're always the same. It's some guy

asking me out. He won't give his name or say who gave him mine. He always says his friend told him I was 'real cute.' "

"Any idea who it is?" Brendan asks.

I shake my head. "Sometimes I think that my brother might know something. Like maybe some guy got my name and number from him. But that's dumb. Why would he do that?"

Brendan doesn't say anything. I can't quite believe I've told him.

I force a smile. "Just a dumb joke anyway, right?"

"I've had a few calls like that," Brendan says. "Some guy pretending to ask me out, pretending he's serious."

"You mean Kale and Jason ask you out?" I can't help but laugh, a nervous laugh.

"Not them. Some other fool." He looks at me with a ghost of a smile. "Now, if it were Randy asking me out, I might consider it."

"You like him, don't you?" I am shy, treading ground I have hardly considered before.

"Yeah, I like him. You're blushing, Susan."

The nervous giggles are threatening. "I'm sorry. All this stuff is so new. When you're fat, you're not supposed to think about guys. Or talk about them."

"Yeah, and at Wayne High, if you're gay, you better . . ." Brendan hesitates. "You better pretend you're not."

"How does everyone know you're gay? I hear all these stories about you. I can't believe they're all true."

"The stories aren't true," he says. "I had a semi-kind-of thing going with one guy, and that's as much as I've done. My sort-of-used-to-be boyfriend is the one who spreads most of the rumors, I think."

"He goes here?" I ask.

"Yeah, he goes here." Brendan smiles to himself, a private smile.

"Well . . ." I take a deep breath. I like him so much and I don't want to say the wrong thing. "Why would someone spread rumors like that about you if they're gay too?"

"He's not gay, he thinks. I must be the one; it has to be me. You understand that?"

I shake my head, watching him, the way the sun touches the rich brown of his hair.

"Sophomore year he was this new kid. We had PE together, and we were always looking at each other. One day he asked me to go home with him after school. I did, and we messed around. We got together one time after that, but then he got scared. He was this big jock, and he couldn't handle it. He's the one who started the petition, I think."

I am horrified. "But you could have told about him, that he was gay too."

Brendan looks at me. "No. I couldn't have done that. Not because I'm so noble, but who would have believed me? I thought that if I kept quiet, the whole thing would go away."

"But it didn't."

"The guy is Justin Wright," he says. "Tracee's boyfriend. I hope Randy beats him out for quarterback next year."

The look on Brendan's face registers before the information. He is hurting.

"I won't say anything, Brendan."

"I know you won't."

"I like you," I tell him. "I think you're about the most interesting person I've ever met."

Brendan smiles at that. "Watch out, Susan. I'm tempted to use the *S*-word."

I look at him, puzzled, then laugh. "Not *sweet!*"

"With you it's unavoidable."

I duck my head, staring at my hands. Inside I am buzzing, alive.

17
EARLY MORNING/ SPRING VACATION

DAD JOGS EVERY MORNING. TOM USED TO GO WITH him some days, to the high school track at 6 A.M. Not so much now. I am looking to exercise more. I am looking to communicate with Dad. Late Sunday night, the week of spring vacation, I decide to ask next morning if I can go along with him.

I am awake most of the night, afraid I will oversleep and miss the moment. In the end I drift off and wake with a start just before my alarm goes off at five-thirty.

I see a light burning downstairs, in the front room. Dad is in front of the picture window, doing windmills. Benny is sitting on one of the armchairs, watching him. I can't help but laugh.

"Hey, Susie," Dad says, turning around. "What are you doing up? Anything wrong?"

"No." I am suddenly shy, moving to the chair to rub Benny's head. He looks at me, motor loud.

"I was wondering if I could go to the track with you." I look away at Dad's silence. "I know I couldn't keep up or anything, but I thought the exercise might be good."

Dad begins to move again, stretching his torso, bringing his left arm, then his right arm, tight across his body. "Are you sure?"

I scoop Benny up and hug him. "I'd like to go."

Dad and I drive over in the SUV. We live close enough to walk to the track, but this will begin his day at Wayne High, from which he will not return till late afternoon at best. It is technically vacation, but Dad always works through the holidays.

"Someone was saying something good about you the other day," Dad tells me as we are locking the car.

"Really?" Groggy, shy, I scuff my toe against the asphalt. "Mr. Duffy? That class is going really well."

He shakes his head, and we fall in step together. "No. One of your real classes. I remember, it was Dennis Haynes, your math teacher. Ran into him in the teachers' lounge and he said he was impressed at your hard work in his class. I was pleased to hear that, Susie."

I shrug, bewildered but happy to take the praise. "I don't mind that class."

"Such enthusiasm," he says, giving me a wink.

I laugh, startled. Maybe the key to Dad is to talk with him before sunrise?

We reach the track and he begins pacing, stretching his legs against the metal railing of the steps that lead to the field. I stretch next to him, self-conscious, my legs so short compared with his. Even at 6 A.M., the Wayne High track sports a few joggers.

Dad hesitates, looking down at me as we stand side by side on the track. "Do you want . . ."

"No," I say, waving at him. "Please just jog, or whatever. I'll do what I can."

He nods. "It's good you're getting the exercise."

I am too embarrassed to jog among these runners, my dad and another man, plus a woman almost as tall and slim as my father. I stay on the outer edge of the track and walk, determined to stay the distance as long as my dad is jogging.

He runs effortlessly, his long legs flashing in green warm-up pants. Six miles he runs, twenty-four laps around the track. I don't make that, but I walk half as many, twelve times around, three miles. My legs are aching at the end, I am breathing hard, but I feel satisfied. Proud of myself. I daydream what it might be like to exercise for real, every day, in the right clothes, not jeans and a T-shirt.

Dad pulls alongside. I am back at the railing, leaning, sweating. He sweats too, breathing hard.

"Okay, hon. Unless you want a lift back, I'm going to walk over to the locker room and grab a shower."

"I can walk home, no problem." Not too many fat-bashers out before eight, I think. I hope. "Dad, you want to walk one last lap with me?"

He wipes the heel of his hand across his forehead. "How many did you do?"

I shift. "Twelve, but I thought maybe we could talk or something."

Dad is looking across the football field, toward the locker room. I feel his urge to get away.

"More exercise," I say in a small voice.

He shrugs, gives me a quick smile. "One for the road."

Dad walks fast, distracted. I try to match my pace to his.

"I've been dieting a little," I tell him. He doesn't answer.

"I'd like to start coming to the track with you," I say. "Maybe not every day, but . . ."

"If you can make it up and out by six," Dad says, "you know where to find me."

A few more joggers have joined us. Older men, a few women. Dad nods to them, chats with one or two.

One of the women my dad doesn't greet reminds me of my mom. She is heavy. Determined. Pacing around the edge of the track. Fortyish, the way Mom would have been.

I look at him shyly. "Being here, like this, I like it."

Being with you.

We are almost all the way around.

"I want to thank you for Mr. Duffy's class," I say. "I'm sorry for the trouble, but . . ."

He glances at me. "Mr. Duffy's class is private, Susan, you know that. I hope you're not going around school talking about it."

What, with my million friends?

I shrug, slowing. Dad doesn't bother to slow with me.

"Randy's in it," I say softly.

Your Randy. Your football player. Not a freak.

He looks back at me, frowning, allowing me to catch up. "I'm aware of that. Remember, I want you to keep this private. I know Randy's parents feel the same way."

??? Why, Dad? Why private? What am I doing in Mr. Duffy's class, and why can't we talk about it?

"Is it okay if I come to the track with you in the mornings?" I say. Dad looks toward the gym. "You and Mom used to . . ."

His attention is on me suddenly. "Susan, go home. I'll see you there tonight."

Stung, I turn my back on him and trot down the stairs.

"You can come with me," he calls after. "Anytime." I keep my back tight as I walk away, the insecurity, the longing, the pleasure of movement, and the anger mixed inside me.

———

THINGS I WANT TO TELL YOU
I love Randy Callahan.
Someone is prank-calling me.
Brendan Slater is my friend.
You're too hard on Tom.
I'm afraid of Kale Krasner.
I want to talk about my mother.

18
Heal with Love

IT IS STIFLING HOT—IN THE NINETIES OUTSIDE,
ten degrees more in the trailer. It is our first meeting since spring
vacation, and no one is talking.

Amber sits nearest the door, arms folded, legs crossed, head
down.

Kale is next to her, sitting tight himself.

Tracee is focused on her nails. Patiently, painstakingly, she files
each to a perfect oval, frowning in concentration.

Randy is openly bored, hardly bothering to disguise his yawns.
Seated next to me, he stares out the small cracked window opposite at the field beyond.

Brendan is on my other side, so I am in heaven. Happy to be
back at school, a first. I keep to the vibe of the room and sit as
sullen as the others.

Mr. Duffy sighs. "What is this, gang? You are dead today."

Randy shifts his attention. "Mr. Duffy, be a good guy and let us
go early. It's too hot for anything else."

"Nope." Mr. Duffy smiles. "You're going to get your money's

worth out of each class." No reaction. "All right, how about this: sex!"

Everyone looks at him.

"What about sex?" Kale says, cracking his knuckles.

Mr. Duffy shrugs, showing off the spreading half-moons of sweat under his arms. "You tell me."

"Be careful," Amber says. "You don't talk about that stuff at school."

"You don't, huh? I'll bet there isn't one of you that doesn't talk sex every day. You're teenagers, aren't you?"

"That is a stereotype," Tracee says, her legs crossed.

My lips are clamped. My closest connection to sex is sitting next to me, Randy Callahan, and that link exists safe only in my mind.

Mr. Duffy is holding back a smile. "No one in this room has any interest in sex? I don't believe it."

"Not in talking about it," Randy mutters.

"Let's get theoretical then," Mr. Duffy says. "When should a boy have sex for the first time? Randy?"

"I don't know." Randy pulls out of his slouch. "My answer is different from my parents', probably."

"Try us," Tracee says.

"Okay. I'm supposed to say 'When he gets married.' But the guys I know, my friends and me, we'd probably say fifteen, sixteen maybe."

"What about a girl?" Mr. Duffy says. "First time."

Randy groans. "Mr. Duffy, please. Ask Tracee."

"I'm asking you," Mr. Duffy says.

"Okay, eighteen or nineteen. Or when she gets married, I suppose."

"Now wait a minute," Tracee says. "That is not fair."

Out of the corner of my eye I see Mr. Duffy grinning. He has engaged us.

"Hey, Trace, if you think it should be earlier . . ." Randy sits back to watch her.

"Men and women should both wait till they're married. It's not fair for you to say a guy should do it at fifteen—"

"Or sixteen, I said."

"And a girl should wait. Who's the guy supposed to do it with?"

"Some slut," Kale drawls. Tracee shudders and pointedly looks away from him.

"Susan?" Mr. Duffy peers at me. "What do you think?"

I shrink. Isn't it obvious I don't have a stake in this?

"Why ask her?" Kale knows. "You might as well ask Slater when a girl should lose it."

Brendan quick-taps my thigh with his. "We're all virgins here." He glances at Randy. "Most of us, anyway. I make do with my imagination. I'll bet Susan does too."

I can't help but laugh, burning face and all.

Kale stares at us. "What's that supposed to mean?"

"Sorry to disappoint you, but my sex life is pretty nonexistent." Brendan's voice is cold and hard. "Worry about your own, if you have one."

"You watch your mouth, fag." Kale is on his feet.

"Sit down," Mr. Duffy says. He is standing along with Kale.

"Sit down, Krasner." Randy sounds bored.

A pause. Then Kale folds back into his chair. "Slater can't cut me like that," he says, glaring at Mr. Duffy. "If I can't cut him, he can't cut me."

Brendan laughs a little, just a little, in the back of his throat. I sense that he is about to say something more, something sarcastic. I reach over to him. I put my hand over his. Brendan's hand is trembling slightly.

"What's that?" Kale shouts, pointing at us. "You two going out now?"

I leave my hand where it is.

"Lynzie Dolan said Susan and Slater eat lunch together every day now." It is Amber. She is awake, eyes bright, hair pushed back to take in the view. This is my protector from Tracee?

"We do, Amber," I say, cutting. "Shocking, isn't it?"

She stares at me, then smiles. "Not so shocking."

"Brendan, what did you mean about Kale's interest in your sex life?" Mr. Duffy's words are measured. He is looking at Kale, not Brendan, as he speaks.

Brendan nods to me and I pull my hand back, exhilarated.

Something real.

"He calls me," Brendan says. "Him and his friend Schrader. They call and according to them, I'm the whore of Wayne High. Kind of funny, really."

No one laughs. Randy clears his throat. Kale is shaking his head.

"No way," he mumbles. "No way."

"That is so wrong," Tracee says, fiddling with her purse strap. "I don't approve of homosexuality either, but harassing someone isn't going to make them change."

"I ain't called no one," Kale says.

Tracee raises her eyebrows. "Do you mean you haven't called anyone? I don't believe that for a second."

Kale stands, shoving his chair back so it skids halfway to the wall. "Think you're better than me." He is sputtering. "Well, fuck you all!"

I close my eyes to avoid his, trying to swallow past the lump in my throat.

When I look again, Kale is gone.

"He's out now, right?" Tracee is smiling.

Mr. Duffy is quiet a moment. "I hope not. I want him here."

Tracee throws up her hands. "After what he's said to you, to me, to all of us? Any other teacher would have thrown him out weeks ago."

"It should be clear by now that I don't believe in throwing anyone out. The discussion ends that way, but the problem doesn't."

Tracee opens her mouth and shuts it like a fish.

Mr. Duffy regards her a moment. "I'm going after him."

Tracee waits until he is gone, then goes to the door. She peers outside and shuts it to face us.

"Everyone. Listen. He can't bring Kale back. Let's get together on this."

"You and Kale have something in common," Brendan says.

Tracee returns to her seat. "Please, don't insult me."

Brendan's smile might as well be painted on wood. "He hates gays, you hate gays."

"What?" She places a hand to her chest. "I said I disapprove of homosexuality. I didn't say anything about hate."

"What's the difference between hate and disapproval? I really want to know."

Tracee's brow is furrowed. "In my church, we hate the sin, not the sinner. We don't hate homosexuals; we heal them with love."

"That's ugly stuff." Brendan's voice is tight.

"Oh, Brendan," Tracee says. "You're not listening."

"No, you aren't."

She sits back. "Are you saying the rumors are true? That you really are gay?"

Amber laughs. "You're a quick study, Ellison."

"But . . ." Tracee looks at the rest of us. "Brendan said he's a virgin. How can he be gay if he's a virgin?"

"You're a virgin, aren't you, Tracee?" Brendan stares at her. "You're into the Bible and all that. You have to be a virgin."

"That's right," Tracee says.

Brendan takes a deep breath. "Are you waiting for your first time to find out if you're gay or straight?"

Amber snorts laughter. "Good one, Slater."

"Come on," Tracee says, dividing a glare between Brendan and Amber. "That is not the same thing."

"Why not?" Brendan says. "Did you wake up one day and say, 'Hey, I like guys!'? Or did you just know?"

Tracee hesitates. "That's the normal thing, isn't it?"

"Normal for you," Brendan says.

The outside steps begin to shake and I know Mr. Duffy is on his way in. When the door opens, I see that Kale is with him.

They come in together. Mr. Duffy leaves the door open, and he and Kale stand next to it, almost outside the trailer.

"Kale has something to say," Mr. Duffy announces. "Then he's out for the day."

"Well, we can't wait to hear it," Tracee says, sugar and scorn mixed.

Kale is head down. "Sorry for swearing and, um . . . getting rude before. I want to stay in this class. If I get kicked out of here, I get kicked out of school. My mom'll take my truck and I'll probably have to go to continuation next year. There's some guys there who want to beat me up."

"None of that is our problem," Tracee tells him.

"I can't talk good like the rest of you," Kale says, "but I don't mind listening. Just back off me," he adds, sounding more like himself. "I don't go after no one who don't go after me first."

Lie. Total lie.

Fat Bitch.

Fat Bitch hates you, Krasner.

I am almost ready to speak up, to say why I don't believe Kale deserves yet another chance. I stare at Mr. Duffy, my throat dry as I anticipate the words.

Brendan's leg presses against mine. I look at him. He shakes his head slightly, eyes liquid.

117

I take a breath and lose my momentum. Lose my will to speak against Kale.

"You have a tough decision to make," Mr. Duffy tells us after Kale leaves. "I want him back, but not unless all of you agree."

I shudder. Tracee catches it.

"Susan's afraid of Kale," she says, "and I can see why. He threatened me; he threatened all of us. I think he's dangerous."

"Why don't you heal him with love, Tracee?"

I hardly recognize Brendan, the focused near-hate on his face. I think of Justin, and how he is in the room between them and Tracee doesn't know.

"What are you talking about?" Tracee's voice is hushed.

"If you really believe in that Bible, you can't pick and choose," Brendan says. "Isn't the big thing to love your enemies? If anyone needs to be healed, it's Kale. Not me."

"Tracee," Mr. Duffy says, "this may be the first time Kale has ever had to think about what he's doing. Really face it. Can you see his presence here as an opportunity?"

"Mr. Duffy, that is not fair," Tracee says. "We're sitting here like lab rats. Why do we have to put up with Kale Krasner while he does or does not change?"

"Why not you?" Mr. Duffy says. "If not here, where? You could be the ones to save him."

"See, Tracee?" Brendan's voice is soft. "Heal with love."

She bridles. "Fine. Mr. Duffy, if you want him back, I won't fight it."

"Either way's all right by me," Randy says.

"Amber?" Mr. Duffy says.

She shrugs. "Yeah, bring him back."

"Brendan?"

"Bring him on."

"Susan?"

"Say yes," Brendan mouths to me. More than once.

I am scared. I trust Brendan. And I am curious too. "Okay, Mr. Duffy," I say. "Bring Kale back."

19
ANOTHER CALL

THAT NIGHT, DAD IS AT WAYNE HIGH'S MONTHLY board meeting.

Tom is staying over at Scott's.

I am doing my homework, Mr. Haynes's first, in honor of his compliment.

At 9 P.M. the phone rings.

I pick up and say nothing.

He doesn't either.

We wait. He gives first.

"Hi, uh, is this Susan?" he says.

My grip tightens on the phone. It's him. The mystery man.

Kale-connected?

"Susan?"

Nothing.

"Yeah." He clears his throat. "A friend of mine gave me your number. He goes to Wayne High with you. Says you're a real cute girl and I should call you."

I take shallow breaths, not wanting him to hear even that.

"Want to go out sometime? You don't know me, but . . ."

He stops. I have not spoken, have not supplied my cue for him to tell me how cute I sound over the phone.

"Anyway. Susan? You alone?"

I push disconnect quietly, my finger barely a press against the button. I set the receiver down. Benny, comfortable on the table, paws tucked, stretches his neck to sniff the phone.

I smile, giving him a cheek stroke with one finger. "Back to work, boy," I tell him, picking up my pencil.

20
FREAKY LUNCH

STUDENTS ARE NOT SUPPOSED TO EAT LUNCH IN THE football bleachers. Brendan and I try it once and it becomes our place. We always take the long way around, so we won't be spotted, through the abandoned basketball courts on the hill overlooking Wayne High. Only a rusted railing divides the courts from the top of the bleachers, and we duck under, perching near the top of the steps to eat, in a corner shadowed by overhanging brush.

I describe my latest call. Brendan doesn't see my triumph. He looks away as I finish.

I'm disappointed. "Don't you think it's good, that I didn't talk to him? Before I always thought I had to."

"Why do they think it's such an insult?" he says, turning to me. "The idea of us going out with anyone?"

I pop my Diet Coke. "I don't know. Like we'd want to go out with them anyway."

Brendan shakes his head. "You are a cute girl, Susan." I make a face, half pleased, half embarrassed.

The brush behind us crackles wildly and Brendan swears, swinging around. I hunch forward, afraid to look.

"This where the freaky people eat?"

Sounds like Amber. I turn to watch as she emerges from the fenced-off grove of trees directly behind the bleachers. Knee-high weeds, still green this time of year, grab at her jeans.

"Who's with you?" Brendan says. His voice is unsteady.

Amber pushes back a ruffle of black hair. She is sweating, carrying a paper bag, her backpack hanging off one shoulder. "Susan, hold the fence for me, will you?"

To Brendan's frown, I move up a step to pull the gap in the fence wider so she can squeeze through. Amber doesn't smell too good—a mix of sweat and beer. But I see that her bag holds Doritos and a Pepsi.

"Thanks," she tells me, settling one step up from us. "So, can I eat with you guys?" Irony in her voice.

Brendan says it. "You setting us up for something? Who was in the woods with you?"

She stares at him, a laser stare through mascaraed eyes. "The Wayne High Wildcats. We were having a time."

"That's not what I meant," Brendan says.

"I don't have the energy," Amber says. "I'm about as in-demand as the two of you."

"Brendan, I think it's okay," I tell him. "Let her eat with us."

Amber looks down into her sack. "Yeah, please," she whispers, two syllables on the *please*.

Brendan doesn't answer, just shakes his head. He turns his back on her and digs into his lunch.

She crunches away, eating fast. I hear her chug-a-lug the Pepsi. I pick at my Wheat Thins and carrot sticks, still a little embarrassed to eat in front of a stranger.

When Amber is finished, she leaves, just leaves—no good-bye, her bag crumpled to the ground next to the empty Pepsi bottle.

She doesn't eat with us again. But something has changed.

21
She Said Stuff

"I beat up Meredith Nelson for talking shit about me," Amber says at the next session. "That's why I'm here. Anyone else want to spill?"

Deep silence.

"How about you, Ellison?" Amber stares at Tracee. "Did you break a nail and swear, or what?"

Tracee stops her manicure. "Who's Meredith Nelson?" she asks with a cool shrug.

"I know her," I say. "We had PE together last year."

Amber turns to me. "What did you think of her?"

I remember a small girl, dumpy, loud with her two friends in class, quiet with the rest of the group. "I don't know. Just average, I guess."

"We used to be friends," Amber says. "She flipped on me, and I made her pay."

I nod, a little scared. Intrigued too.

"Real brave," Tracee says. "You beat up some girl because you didn't like what she said?"

Amber smiles. "I sent her to the hospital."

"That was you?" Tracee's voice is hushed. "I remember hearing about that, two girls fighting after school." She turns to Mr. Duffy. "Why is Amber in here with us? What I did was nowhere near that."

"You're here for a reason," Mr. Duffy says, severe for him.

"Meredith needed a few stitches, is all," Amber says. "She scraped her hand when I knocked her down. I scared her off campus. She's on home study, last I heard."

"You think that's something to brag about?" Tracee looks around at the rest of us.

"She was doing something to hurt me, and I stopped her," Amber says. "That's not bragging. It's taking care of business."

"Taking care of business," Kale mumbles, the first time he has spoken in class since we voted him back in.

"Amber," Tracee says, "why beat Meredith up? Why not talk it out with her? She used to be your friend."

"Has anyone ever attacked you, Ellison? With words, I mean?"

Tracee sits back. "Yes! In eighth grade, at the Halloween dance, I danced with this new guy just to be nice. He would not leave me alone after that. He left notes on my desk, in my locker, he called me at home until my dad yelled at him. Then he wrote stuff about me in the boys' bathroom, and other guys started to hit on me because of that."

"So what did you do?" Amber asks.

"I was going out with Josh Denair then; he was a freshman here. He got a bunch of his friends and they beat the guy up."

Amber says what I am thinking. "You got them to do your job for you. At least I fight for myself."

"You're a girl," Tracee says. "And you beat up another girl. That's just low-class. I'm sorry, but it is."

"Meredith says stuff and I'm supposed to take it? Sit down and discuss it with her? She wouldn't understand that."

"Whatever." Tracee is on nail patrol again.

"What she was saying, half of it was lies." Amber looks at us, searching. "I had to stop her. Randy? Kale? Did she get to you guys?"

Kale doesn't answer. Randy shifts. "Amber, forget it," he says.

"What did Meredith say?" Tracee sounds so patient. So patronizing.

"Maybe none of you know," Amber says. "Maybe all of you do." Her gaze flicks over Brendan and me.

I look at Amber closely. Face pale as paper, eyes ringed by mascara and dark circles, she doesn't look well.

"I haven't heard a thing about you," Tracee says. She is smirking. "Not a thing."

Amber's a slut.

Amber's a skank.

Amber can kick your ass.

Whatever it is, is bad. I glance at Brendan. He is frowning.

———

I AM NOT SURE WHAT I AM DOING. I AM NOT SURE why.

Amber is first out after class, and I am second. I follow as she walks swiftly past the tennis courts.

I am panting before long, pacing myself against her long legs. She stops and I don't notice until I am close to running into her.

"What do you want?" she says, scowling, looking past me toward the trailer. "Come on, then, walk with me."

We stop halfway up the service vehicle driveway between the Humanities complex and the old classroom building.

"What do you want?" she says more gently.

"I don't know. I felt bad about what happened in class. The way Tracee was treating you."

"Don't worry about Ellison," she says. "I'm going to get her."

I take a step back. "You aren't going to hurt her, are you?"

"Not like Meredith, no. What do you care? You think Tracee Ellison cares about you?"

"I know she doesn't." Once I say it, I know it's true.

"The blonde hair, the big eyes—not much else is going on there, Susan."

"You don't know that," I say automatically. Then I remember who I'm talking to. "Sorry."

"Don't apologize. You see everyone's side, don't you?"

I shrug, embarrassed. "Everyone but Kale's, I guess."

"There's your guy," Amber says lightly, gesturing behind. I turn and see Brendan at the driveway entrance, watching us. "He's worried about you."

"I'm okay," I say. "How about you?"

"I saw you checking me out in class. I look like shit today, don't I?"

Honesty. "Yeah. Is something wrong?"

"What if I tell you I'm pregnant, but I won't be after today?" Amber spreads her hands across her belly. "What would you say to that?"

I think about it. "I'd say I'm sorry. I'd say it's your business."

Amber moves toward me. I resist—just—the urge to retreat. "You won't tell anyone? Not even your boyfriend?"

I don't bother with the "boyfriend" denials. We both know what she means. "I won't tell anyone."

She regards me for a long moment, then smiles. "Thanks."

I return her smile. "You're welcome."

22
SEEING ME

BRENDAN AND I WALK AROUND A CORNER, AND MY
brother and his friends are ranged out along the redbrick walls,
laughing about something even before they see us.

Tom takes us in first and looks at me, furious. I meet his look
and hold it until he turns away. I see the impulses warring in the
rest of the boys. Brendan is irresistible; as Tom's sister, I am off-
limits. Bowing slightly, Scott gestures us through. Some of the
guys laugh. One of them clicks his tongue, another hisses a sigh,
but none of them says anything as we pass.

——

"WHAT DO YOU THINK YOU'RE DOING WITH THAT
guy?" Tom asks later, perched on the couch, baseball game muted
in the background.

I am in the easy chair, legs tucked under, doing my grammar
homework. Legs tucked under and I can *breathe*: Mom's jeans
are starting to feel loose.

"The same things you do with your friends," I tell him.

"What do you mean?" He is staring at me. Seeing me.

"I walk with Brendan, and we talk, and we laugh. He's my friend."

"He's a freak." Tom emphasizes the last word, coming down hard on the *k.*

I pull my shoulders in. "So am I, then."

"Don't be so dramatic. You think it's going to help you to hang around with him?"

I look at him. "Yeah, I do."

"Dad won't like it," Tom warns.

"Dad won't care," I say, but my stomach twists.

Tom turns to the TV, popping the volume on. "You're going to embarrass yourself," he says, distant now. "You know what people say about him."

"I know Brendan gets treated like dirt." I am starting to get angry. "Just like me."

Tom sighs. "Please."

How could you let your friends treat me like that? Treat me and my friend that way?

The words are so close, so loud in my head, that for a moment I feel I have said them. But no.

"Tom, do you ever miss her?" I say, too loud, over the TV noise. Needing him to hear me.

He doesn't answer. It is Dad's trick: Pretend you don't hear and it will go away, whatever it is you are trying to lose.

"Mom," I say, still loud. "I've been thinking about her. Her birthday's next month. She would have been forty-two."

Stone silence. Tom works his jaw. He punches the volume on the remote and the game noise rises by two.

"I was thinking about calling Aunt Cecile, just to talk," I tell him. "Remember when we stayed with her that time? It was fun, wasn't it?"

"No." Tom looks like a turtle the way he turns his head to me without moving his body. "No, it wasn't fun, because I was worried about Mom. Weren't you?"

The English text is heavy on my lap. I close it, my homework stuck inside to mark the place.

"Yes, I was worried." But I remember the ranch mostly, riding horses, watching Aunt Cecile paint, playing with her cats.

"Think about someone besides yourself," Tom says, lip curled. "Whatever you're doing with Slater, it's going to double back on you. And me."

"I'm going upstairs," I tell him, gathering my things.

I stop at the edge of the room. "You know Mom didn't want us to worry about her, Tom. You know she didn't."

I get nothing back, not even a grunt.

23

KALE KALE KALE

AMBER IS LATE NEXT SESSION. SHE TAKES A SEAT next to Kale, spreading a glare at the rest of us staring.

Mr. Duffy clears his throat. "Kale, you're in the spotlight today. I want to hear something positive from you. I want to hear some positive things about you."

Kale goes squinty. "What the . . . ?"

"You don't have to do a thing but listen, to start," Mr. Duffy says. "I want everyone to share one nice thing about Kale."

Tracee is directly across from me. We catch each other's appalled expressions. She smiles at me, rolls her eyes Kale's way.

"Hey!" Kale says. "I saw that. I'm not taking her stuff."

"Now, wait," Mr. Duffy says. "Let's get into the spirit of this, shall we? Tracee, please."

She sighs. "Mr. Duffy, I don't believe in cutting people. Pass."

"You see!" Kale says.

"We'll come back to you, Tracee," Mr. Duffy says. "Let's go around the room. Amber? Let's hear something positive about Kale."

"He's all right," she says. A long thirty seconds of silence ticks off.

"Come on, Amber." Kale attempts a laugh. "More?"

"Kale's mother used to baby-sit me when I was little," she says, "at her day care. We used to play Avalanche and Candy Land, me and Kale and the other kids. It was fun."

"Yeah!" Kale sounds eager. "I forgot about that."

"Brendan?" Mr. Duffy says next.

"No comment."

"Think hard," Mr. Duffy says. "Think creatively."

Brendan sits back and surveys Kale.

"Don't look at me, boy!" Kale says.

Brendan shrugs, looking at Mr. Duffy. "What can I say?"

"Let's be generous here." Mr. Duffy sounds desperate. "Susan?"

I have a memory. It is more of my mom than Kale.

"Who is that little boy?" she asks as we enter the fourth-grade classroom. It's the first day of school for me, the first day of work for her.

She is nodding toward Kale Krasner, who stands alone, staring out the window. He should be in fifth. The other kids are either at their desks or gathered around the teacher at the board.

"It's Kale Krasner." I hit his name hard, and Kale turns. "They held him back," I say, brave with my mom next to me.

I expect him to say something mean or do something nasty. Instead he gives the two of us the look of a lost puppy.

She adopts him that year, and Kale leaves me alone through fourth grade, in the class, at recess, on the bus.

I close my eyes for a moment, remembering. That year, I didn't hate him.

"Kale and I were in the same class," I say, "in fourth grade. Once during free time I was drawing pictures of dogs, and he came over and said I was a good artist."

"You remember that?" Kale is talking to me like I am human. I look at him. Without fear. "Sure. I was pretty shy and it was nice to hear something good about myself."

And nice-bizarre, coming from you.

I think I have struck Kale speechless. His face is reddening. He is scratching his forearms and staring at the floor.

"Mrs. Callaway," I say softly. "She was the aide that year, remember? She helped you learn to read. She was always talking about you."

Kale looks up, face distorted, red-angry now. I sit back.

"I knew how to read!" he says. "That was your mother, wasn't it? She was just as fat as you are. Fatter! She could barely squeeze her ass into one of those little chairs to sit next to me."

I am shocked. I realize how my armor has been chipped away over these weeks. The words are like darts. All I can do is stare at him.

"Krasner, you waste!" Brendan says, as loud as I've ever heard him.

"You don't talk about people's mothers like that," Randy says.

Tracee leans my way. "Don't listen to him, Susan. He is pure trash."

Kale is grinning, leaning against the wall, chair in the air.

He likes being hated. He likes it. That's who he is.

Mr. Duffy nods to me. "Susan, try to answer him."

I clear my throat. "Kale, what did I say to make you mad? I know you didn't hate my mother. Why do you hate me?"

"I don't hate you," he says. "What are you talking about?"

My heart is thumping. "You do these rotten things to me. Always. The second Wednesday of this group, you followed me afterward and asked to come to my house to use the phone. When I said no, you pretended to hit me and called me a fat bitch."

"Nice narc," Kale says. "Never happened."

"You should have told me at the time, Susan." Mr. Duffy is stern.

I shake my head. "No. I'm not saying this to get him in trouble. I'm wondering WHY."

"When does the positive stuff come in, Mr. D?" Kale's grin is sickly.

"It came, and you missed it," Amber says. "Now listen to her."

I am staring at Kale. "All the stuff in elementary school. In fifth grade one day I wore my hair in pigtails, and you sat behind me on the bus and pulled my head back and forth all the way to school."

Kale shrugs. "I don't remember that. Did you tell me to stop?"

I am back in that day, the fear swirling in my throat as Kale snaps my head from side to side. Tom is three seats up, staring ahead even as I catch his eyes in the driver's mirror.

Brendan brings me back with a steady look.

Keep going.

I take a deep breath. "In seventh grade, in choir, you would stand behind me in the risers and change the lyrics to the songs. You sang mean stuff about me being fat."

"If I did, it wasn't personal," Kale says. "I was probably trying to make my friends laugh."

"Then in freshman year, you—"

"What do you want me to say?" Kale emphasizes each word. "You're sounding like my mother here. You want me to say I'm a creep loser? Maybe I am. So?"

"Why'd you say that stuff about my mom?"

"I knew how to read!" Kale's face flames. "What, did she go home and tell you I couldn't? Maybe I am dumb, but she didn't have to say it."

I shake my head. "Kale, no. I don't remember exactly what my mom said about you, but it was nothing bad. She liked you. A lot. I was jealous of how much."

Kale flips his hat off and runs a hand through his hair. "This is bullshit," he mutters. "Okay, I'm sorry. Sorry, sorry, sorry."

"Then why?" I say softly. "I want to know why."

"Why I pick on you?" He glances at me, then looks away. "You're fat, and you're alone most of the time. I can do stuff and no one stops me. It's like that. Okay?"

I close my eyes. The room is silent.

"She's not alone anymore," Brendan says. His voice is raspy.

I take a moment to smile at Brendan. "Kale, my mom never said you were dumb. I'm the one who says that." He looks at me. I put a hand to my chest. "In here, every time you say I'm fat, I say you're dumb."

"They held me back," he says, bleak. "My friends moved on. I

137

was eleven years old in fourth grade. Your mom cared about you, didn't she? I know she died. I'm sorry about that."

"Yes," I say. "Thank you."

He nods. "I liked her. I didn't care if she was fat."

"She liked you," I tell him. I am speaking for Mom. I don't like Kale and never will.

I am exhausted. Kale looks worn too. But there is one more thing I have to ask.

"Kale," I say, "do you know who's been prank-calling me?"

He looks at me straight-on. "I never called you. None of my friends did either, far as I know."

I hardly recognize Kale's face unguarded. He is telling the truth, I think. Yet it is not enough.

"This doesn't solve anything," I say, almost to myself. "What he did, it isn't going away. No matter what happens here."

"No," Mr. Duffy agrees softly. "But it is better, isn't it?"

I look at him. I'm not crying, but it is close.

Thank you.

24
JOGGING AROUND

DAD LEAVES THE HOUSE AT SIX O'CLOCK EACH MORN-
ing for his jog. Most days I am with him. I have come to know the
track regulars: a tall, thin older couple; a short, Marine-looking
guy; a heavy middle-aged lady. They exchange nods with Dad,
with me, and keep moving. We do the same, Dad running, me
walking.

It is almost May, a Sunday, and we are halfway through our
routine when I see three teen guys jog onto the track. I freeze for
a moment, anticipating ridicule. I look again. One of the boys is
Randy Callahan, another Justin Wright, and the third I don't
know. I have seen him around school, big, blocky, laughing, always
with a group of jocks.

Disaster, in any case. My head sinks and I continue my march,
joyless now.

Soon enough I hear feet pounding behind me. I brace myself,
but the three pass without comment. Shyly, I watch them go. Justin
is in the middle, taller and leaner than Randy and the other boy.
Better-looking, technically, than Randy, his features finer, but not
more attractive to me. He is Dad's Justin, the quarterback;

Tracee's Justin, the boyfriend; Brendan's Justin, the betrayer. Here just another body pounding around the track. One who has left me alone.

They reach Dad and greet him; Justin runs with him, but Randy and the other boy settle into a steady jog. I relax and count my laps in my head, on seven, anticipating twelve.

The third time Randy passes me, split now from the other boy, he calls over, "Hey, Susan!"

I only stumble a little. "Hey, Randy."

He slows, jogging in place, almost, to let me catch up to him.

"I'm not very fast," I say, glancing at him, sweat flattening my curls.

He grins. "I'm not either. I'm pitiful trying to keep up with Justin. Coach is faster than me too."

We look to the other side of the track, where Dad and Justin are eating up the miles. They have passed me four times, silently; I have counted.

I wait for him to take off, but Randy stays.

"How long you been doing this?" he asks, jogging slowly as I walk fast.

"Oh, a couple of weeks, I guess." I am tense, waiting for some kind of fall; they wouldn't attack with Dad here, and Randy wouldn't attack at all, I think, but it is still me, Susan Callaway, sharing the track with three teenage guys.

"I need to get out more myself," Randy says. "I don't do enough in the off-season."

"You don't go out for baseball, huh?"

"Nah." Randy is frowning. "I told Dad I was dropping baseball once I got to high school. I don't think he believed me."

"Your brother," I say, glancing at him, "he's . . . did he like baseball?"

"He does like baseball," Randy says. "He's the reason Dad wanted me to go on, I think. So I could entertain Kevin."

"I still have the cat," I blurt. "The one you saved. Remember? In Axle Park?"

Randy doesn't answer. He looks over and nods once, awkwardly.

His running companion comes up suddenly and gives him a push. Randy stumbles and I shy to the side.

"Stop making time," the guy says, looking me over, grinning.

I look him over. He is a few inches shorter than Randy, muscle-fat, shorthaired and mean-eyed. I think I know him.

"Are you Eddy?" I ask, cool. I am proud of myself.

His glance shifts. "C'mon, Callahan, this is boring. Let's get out of here." Eddy, Eddy Rogers I remember now, thumbs sideways to where Dad and Justin run. "Let Mr. Perfect run it out with the hard-ass."

"Yeah, okay," Randy says quickly. He nods to me. "Susan."

As the two jog off together, I hear Randy say, "That's his daughter." Eddy shrugs, speeding up a bit, lumbering. He recedes to nothing in my view, but I stay with Randy until he has disappeared down the steps to the main campus.

—

Dad and I go to breakfast afterward. Denny's, again.

"Those guys at the track," I say. "They're your players, aren't they?"

Dad focuses on me. "Sure. Wright, Callahan, and Rogers. They need to work harder, all three of them. I keep telling them they need to run."

"Randy Callahan." I look down. "He's really good, you think?"

I like him, Dad. I like him a lot. I know he doesn't like me like that; he couldn't. But maybe as a friend?

"Randy Callahan is lazy." Dad's voice is crisp. "He's a kid who needs pushing."

The waitress comes and takes our orders. When she's gone, Dad mentions Randy again. "Don't get me wrong," he says. "That kid has potential. How many did he get in today? Did you count?"

"I don't know." My skin heats. "I don't watch him that close."

Randy did three laps. Three and a half, I guess. He did half of one with me.

"He was barely there." Dad shakes his head. "That Eddy Rogers either."

"I was worried they'd say stuff," I tell him. "That they'd, you know, make fun of me."

Dad is looking at me like I'm speaking Venusian.

"Randy wouldn't," I add, "but you never know with the others. With any guys, really."

"Susie," he says, in a tone I hardly recognize, "has someone been bothering you?"

We stare at each other. I look away first.

So many for so long, Dad. How can you not know?

"Everything's fine," I say. "Your players . . . the guys . . . they were okay with me."

Pretty okay.

"Of course they were," Dad says lightly. "They'd better be."

We smile past each other.

25
Score

BRENDAN BOUNDS UP THE TRAILER STEPS AND TRIES the door. "Locked. He's back to late."

"Three more meetings," I say. "Can you believe it?"

Brendan and I settle on the top step, taking the sun, not talking.

"Hey," someone says in a gruff voice on the approach.

"Hey, Amber," I say, half turning.

She comes around and leans against the trailer's ridged metal wall. "Did you tell him?" she asks, nodding toward Brendan.

I know at once what she means. "No," I tell her. Brendan looks at me, then stands, moving toward the tennis courts where the games are now in session.

"I did it," Amber says, taking Brendan's spot. "That thing I said I was going to do."

"Oh yeah?" I don't know what to do with Amber's confidence. Are we friends now?

"Right after I talked to you. Feels kind of weird." She looks at me, a hand up to shade her eyes.

What is the right thing to say? "I bet" is judgmental. "No kidding?" sounds sarcastic. "Give me details" is out of the question.

I settle for a nod. Amber watches me another moment, then looks away.

"I'm going to get Ellison today," she says quietly.

Before I can react, Brendan is in front of us. "They're coming," he says. "Mr. Duffy and everyone."

In the trailer Amber takes the seat next to me. I am tense, wondering what she expects of me.

"The swamp cooler is finally kicking in," Mr. Duffy says. "I complained to the janitor, and what do you know? The beast is fixed."

It is true. For the first time in weeks, the trailer is comfortable.

Kale is looking at me. I meet his gaze and I'm surprised when he gives me a nod. I can't quite form a smile, but I return his nod.

All is forgiven? That easy?

I am confused. Next to me, Brendan scowls.

"I have a topic," Mr. Duffy says. "Unless someone else wants to start us off."

"I will," Amber says. "I want to talk about guys. The way they use girls and throw them away."

"Here we go," Randy says.

"Yeah, here we go." Amber stares at him until he meets her eyes. "You ready?"

He looks away, scanning past my face, expressionless.

"Girls let themselves be used," Tracee says. "Girls set the tone. Make your own choices, Amber."

"Thanks for the advice," Amber says. "I do."

"I set limits," Tracee says, her voice level. "My boyfriend and I respect each other. I don't tease Justin, and he doesn't push me."

Brendan sighs very quietly, but Tracee hears and looks at him sharply.

"He lies to you, Tracee," Amber says.

Tracee's mouth drops open.

"All guys do. Nice ones. Assholes. All ages. They lie."

"Like girls never do," Kale says.

Amber looks at him. "Sure we do. I'm talking about guys now."

"You don't know me. Or Justin," Tracee says. She points at Amber. "Speak for yourself."

"I am. Do you think there's a reason he doesn't push you?"

Tracee doesn't respond. She is staring at Amber.

"He drinks, your Justin. Did you know that?"

"Amber, don't," Randy says, low.

"I see him at parties," Amber says. "That's where I first got to know him."

"You and Justin don't go to the same parties." Tracee laughs. Short. Sharp.

"Is he with you every weekend, Ellison? Every single weekend?" Amber hits the words hard.

"Whatever lie you're pushing, just say it." Tracee's words are ice.

Amber waits. Looks around the circle. Then nods. "There are parties in the country, a couple of times a month, out near the college. Guys rent houses out there. Good music, anything you want to drink. Or smoke. Anything you want."

"Skank affairs," Tracee says. "I'd never go."

"No one's asking you." Amber turns to Mr. Duffy. "I want to

talk about something that happened at one of those parties. What I say can't leave the room."

"What we say here is confidential," Mr. Duffy says. "That's the rule. Everyone understand that?" He waits for our mumbled agreement. "Amber?"

"Okay." She takes a deep breath. "This one party a couple of months ago, I got hammered. More than wasted. The next day I woke up on someone's bedroom floor. I didn't know why I was there or why I was naked."

Tracee looks like she smells something bad.

"At school on Monday, people were laughing at me. Meredith Nelson was the worst. She was the only other girl I knew at the party. She had this stupid smirk every time I saw her. Finally I got her alone. I asked what she was smiling about, and she wouldn't say. I slapped her, and pulled her hair, knocked her down and kicked her—"

"We get it," Tracee says. "So what happened?"

Amber is expressionless. "Meredith said I passed out at the party, and some guy carried me to a bedroom. She said guys went in and out of that room all night."

My hands are cold. What I am thinking is how lonely Amber must have been. How lonely she is now.

me and the Wayne High Wildcats

"Randy?" I say, not sure what I am asking.

He shifts in his chair, legs outstretched, hands in his pockets. "I was there. I saw the guy carry her into the room. Amber, I didn't know you were in trouble. You were kissing him pretty good before."

"Once a slut, always a slut, right?" Amber says.

"No," he says. "I didn't know what to do. That's the truth. I was scared. I left with Justin and Eddy before anything happened."

"Justin?" Tracee puts a hand to her chest. "He was there?"

Amber nods slowly.

"Guys do dumb things sometimes," Tracee says. "What excuse does a girl have for going to a party like that?"

"We don't all have a regulation social life, Ellison." Amber's voice is acid.

Or any social life.

"I'm sorry that happened to you." Tracee is talking fast. "But you shouldn't have been there and you know it. People are responsible for their own mistakes."

Amber nods. "That's what I used to tell Justin whenever he would say what a bitch you are, but he stayed with you anyway. No accounting, I guess."

Kale lets out a wolf whistle.

"You're lying," Tracee says.

"I'm not lying." Amber sounds unexpectedly compassionate. "Justin and I were seeing each other for a while. While he was seeing you. He'd come over some nights my mom was working and we'd talk some, fool around some. Never all the way."

"Lie." Tracee's face is rigid.

"Things changed after the party," Amber says. "He couldn't look me in the face after that. One night he asked me to meet him on the football field. I felt so shitty about myself, I went. When I got there, he had a couple of friends with him."

She waits, but no one has a comment.

"I thought it didn't matter. I thought I didn't care." Amber shrugs. "They pulled a train on me, Tracee. Do you know what that means?"

Kale whistles again, low.

"Of course I know what it means." Tracee sounds afraid, not angry.

"Justin led off," Amber says. "Only he couldn't quite . . . you know. He pretended. I let him pretend. I don't think he appreciated it, though. He hasn't talked to me since."

Brendan laughs, sharp, sudden, like he has been holding it back. He clamps his hand over his mouth. "Sorry, I'm sorry."

"Oh, man." Kale has his face in his hands. "This class is the best!"

Tracee draws herself up, beautiful in her chocolate brown T-shirt and snug beige jeans. "You are a disgusting, slutty whore," she pronounces.

"So's your boyfriend." Amber is defiant, holding strong.

Tracee's face colors white to red. In one graceful move she sweeps up her purse and her books. In another she is out the door.

"Score," Amber says. She sounds sad.

Dead silence. I am afraid to look at any of the guys, including Mr. Duffy. Amber has become another person to me.

"Well," Mr. Duffy says finally. "Anyone have something to add?"

"Justin invited me to the field that night," Randy says. His voice is choked. "I didn't go, but I knew about it."

"I figured," Amber says calmly.

"I'm sorry," Randy says. "I should have . . ." He doesn't finish, eyes downcast.

Amber's face is veiled. "I stayed on the field a long time after they left. I hated myself worse than them. I decided I was never going to be with another guy again unless I loved him. If that guy never comes along, fine." She smiles a little. "Maybe I'll switch teams and join Brendan on the other side."

Brendan smiles at her. "Welcome anytime."

"You're brave, Amber," I tell her. "I think you're brave."

Curtain down. She slumps. "I wish that were enough."

26
Call Me

"I'll probably get another call tonight," I tell Brendan. We are leaning against the top bleacher, lunches finished. It is hot. Far below, on the Wayne High football field, two guys are playing Frisbee, running over and around a quartet of shrieking girls.

"Yeah?" Brendan says, eyes on the action below. "Why tonight?"

I tick off the reasons. "Dad's on a conference. Tom's staying at Scott's. This guy always calls when I'm alone."

"You want me to come over?"

I am suddenly shy. "Come over? You don't have to. Maybe I just won't answer the phone tonight."

"Krasner isn't calling me anymore," Brendan says abruptly. "That's probably because of you, Susan."

"You don't sound very happy about it."

He looks at me. "Like you said, it doesn't solve anything. I want him to know that what he did to me is wrong."

"What did he do, Brendan? Besides the phone calls, I mean. It was more than that, wasn't it?"

Brendan does not respond.

"We got his truck," I say. "Maybe that's enough."

He laughs, a mean laugh. "I got his truck, not you. And he doesn't even know I did it. That's not exactly satisfying."

I am stung. "If Kale knew, he'd hurt you. Maybe bad, with all his friends. He's getting better, can't you see?"

Brendan shakes his head. "It's easier for him to see you and let you go. He still thinks gay people are scum; I know it."

I touch his arm. "Oh, Brendan. What do you care what Kale Krasner thinks of you?"

He doesn't pull away. Instead he sighs, sinking back against the concrete. "What can I say? I care."

"If you want, you can come over tonight," I tell him.

——

BRENDAN'S MOM DROPS HIM OFF AROUND SEVEN. Benny's ears perk up at the sound of an unfamiliar car in the driveway.

I am nervous as I let Brendan in. He is the first friend I have had in the house since Anna in the sixth grade. I have given the place a special cleaning in his honor, but I am still aware of the clutter, and the feeling of disuse that hangs over the house.

Brendan enters warily, looking left, looking right. Then he smiles, and I turn to see Benny watching him from the foot of the stairs.

"This is the great Benny, right?" Brendan says.

"Yeah." I am smiling. "Benny, my friend. He might be shy. . . ."

But Brendan is already stooped, his hand cupped, outstretched. He calls, "Here, kitty." Benny meows a question and trots over. He sniffs Brendan's hand tentatively, then walks past to rub along his leg, tail high.

"He likes you!" I say.

Benny follows us to the kitchen, where I offer Brendan a Mountain Dew.

"We could watch HBO," I say. "Or a video, maybe. We have old stuff, mostly. Black-and-white. My mom liked the oldies."

"I love old movies," Brendan says. "What do you have?"

We are settled in watching *Twelve Angry Men,* eating popcorn, when the phone rings. I don't move, and neither does Brendan, and the caller doesn't leave a message.

I put the movie on pause, ashamed. I look over at Brendan.

"You don't have to answer it," he says. Benny is curled in his lap. "It's your choice."

I shake my head. "I want to resolve this. Please . . . wait in the kitchen with me. He'll call back."

We sit, tense, at the kitchen table. Five minutes go by. Then seven. On eight, the phone rings. Once. Twice. I pick up.

"Hello," I say, voice flat. Brendan is watching me.

"Yeah, hello. Is this Susan?" It's him. Something is different. I close my eyes to concentrate.

"Yes, this is Susan."

"Hi, Susan. A friend gave me your number. He's a good friend of yours, and he says you're a real cute girl. He says we should go out sometime."

I do not respond. I am trying to remember. The voice is suddenly, maddeningly familiar.

"Susan, what do you say? You and me."

"Who's your friend?" I ask, sticking to the script. Buying time.

"He doesn't want his name mentioned. He told me what a good-looking girl you are, someone I should get to know."

"What do you look like?" I ask. A new question from me. I put a little flirt in it, even. Brendan is starting to smile.

The phone guy grunts. "My friends tell me I'm hot."

I laugh. "His friends tell him he's hot."

"No doubt," Brendan says dryly.

Phone Guy clears his throat. "You got someone there, Susan?"

I don't answer.

"So you want to go out? We'd have a good time together, you and me."

"Okay," I say, too loud. "Let's go out." Brendan is grinning.

Phone Guy hesitates. I have moved off the script. Out of my role of Outraged. Pathetic. Scared. Victim.

"Um, my friend says we should go out." Phone Guy sighs. Maybe he can hear how lame he sounds.

"Your friend's right," I tell him. "Let's go out. When and where?"

Silence. In the distance, a giggle. Not Phone Guy's.

"Shut up!" Phone Guy says, not to me. He disconnects.

I listen a moment, then set the phone down. I want to smile, but I am scared to believe.

"Maybe?" I say with a shrug. "You think?"

"Yeah, Susan, you did it." Brendan reaches over and I meet him. We clasp hands, swaying them back and forth over the table, V for victory.

BRENDAN STAYS OVER, DOWNSTAIRS. HE IS THERE in the morning, asleep on the couch, when Tom comes into the kitchen. I am reading the movie section of the *San Francisco Chronicle.*

The look on my brother's face makes me want to laugh, just from sheer punchiness. Laugh, cry, or defend myself—one of those.

"Are you kidding me?" Tom speaks in a kind of strangled whisper. "Brendan Slater isn't really asleep in our living room. Right, Susan?"

I take a sip of cranberry juice. "Right," I say, wiping my mouth with a napkin. "This is all a dream."

Tom grabs a nearly full package of chocolate chip cookies off the counter and a mug from the cabinet and sets them on the table. Then to the fridge for milk, the first time he has looked away from me.

"Scott didn't give you breakfast, huh?" I comment.

He slams down across from me as quietly as a lanky athletic kid can slam. "Yeah. His mom did. I'm still hungry. That okay with you?"

"Whatever." I go back to the paper.

I hear crunching and slurping for the next few minutes. I pretend to read, waiting.

"The cookie packages are lasting longer these days," he says, mouth full.

I look up. "Why do you think that is?"

Tom narrows his eyes. "You dieting?"

"I'm dieting. And exercising. I've lost about ten pounds." Maybe less. I am still afraid of the scale.

"Drop in the bucket," he says. I understand he is scolding me about Brendan, but the words still hurt.

"Got to start somewhere," I say brightly.

"Sorry," Tom says, surprising me. "It's good you're doing that." I wait, scanning him. "Thanks."

"Really, though, why is Brendan Slater here?"

"Why can't you call him 'Brendan'?" I say, my voice lowered, hoping he will follow suit. "Or 'Slater,' if you have to do the jock thing? Calling him by two names is like he's a specimen or something."

"You didn't answer me." Tom's hair sticks up wildly and cookie crumbs dot his lips, stick in his under-lip fuzz.

"You need to shave," I say. "Shower, or something."

"Shave, yeah?" His eyes brighten. I remember Scott calling Tom "Rabbit-Boy" once because of his complexion.

"Brendan's here because I've been getting prank calls," I tell him. "He's here to give me moral support."

"Prank calls?"

Tom is staring at me. I hand a napkin across the table and he wipes his mouth.

"Not dirty calls," I say. "Just . . . cruel. Some guy asking me out. His joke is that no guy would ask me out." I take a deep breath. "I almost recognize the voice. Almost. Is it Scott, do you know? Or one of your other friends?"

My fear, half formed, the one I had hardly allowed myself to consider.

"I don't know who called you," Tom says, looking away. "Don't ask me."

I wait. Something in his voice. "You do know," I say quietly. "You know something."

My brother shakes his head. He won't meet my eyes.

"Your friends laugh at me," I say. "You've seen them do it. You've let them do it. Do they talk about calling me too?"

"I don't like it when the guys rank on you," he says, glancing at me. "I always think if I say something, it'll make it worse. Scott tries to stop them."

"In a smart-ass way." I am angry with Tom, with all of them.

"They wouldn't listen any other way," Tom says. "They wouldn't listen to me at all."

"What about the calls?" I say. "Is it Scott?"

Tom shakes his head. "Scott isn't calling you. He wanted to one day, to play with you a little bit. I told him no."

I feel the tension across my back, the start of a headache pressing at my temples. "That weekend you and him were on the outs. You were so mad at me. What was going on?"

"Scott's mom caught us making prank calls," Tom says. "She said I couldn't come back until I apologized. Until we both apologized."

I am cold all over, but I keep my gaze steady. "Who were you calling?"

"The calls weren't to you," he emphasizes. "Not you. It was

157

Brendan . . . Slater. Scott's mom made me promise to tell Dad, and we both had to write Slater an apology. I didn't want to do it at first. Neither did Scott."

I can't believe what I am hearing. "You didn't tell Dad, right?"

Tom's face twists. "I told him."

"But you didn't write the letter?"

"I wrote it," Tom says. "Mrs. Deschamps took Scott and me to the post office and watched us mail the letters. She read them first."

It's then I remember the piece of paper Tom was trying to hide from me that day.

"Susan?" I look up and see Brendan in the doorway. His face is grave. "I'll be going now."

Tom doesn't turn around, but his shoulders stiffen. He looks to me with a kind of pleading.

"Brendan," I start, and don't know what to add. He comes to the table, ignoring Tom, and I stand. We hug, our first hug, and I press my face against his chest, clean smelling and firm against my cheek.

"Don't lecture me," Tom says the moment the kitchen door closes behind Brendan. "I've heard it all."

"What did Dad say?" I ask, numb.

"He said to handle it myself. Scott's mom gave me hell."

We sit together, slumped in our chairs.

"I barely hang on," Tom says finally, quiet now. "At baseball. In class. With Dad. And you're fat."

He glances at me, and I nod. *Go on.*

"You're fat. And you're friends with Slater. Brendan Slater. You know what they'll say if they find out he spent the night here?"

I am tired. "I can guess. Tell me why I'm supposed to care."

"You don't understand guys." Tom sounds like he is trying to convince himself. "You don't understand the way things work."

"Maybe I don't. But you better get used to it. Brendan's not going anywhere, I hope, so you can just deal with it."

"One of Dad's players might have called you," Tom says after a long pause. "Some of those guys can't stand him."

I laugh. "Like I'm going to tell Dad about this. Like he'd do anything."

"Are you kidding? Dad would go nuts. You should see the way he gets in the locker room if he thinks someone's ranking him."

"I wasn't talking about Dad and his athletes," I say quietly. "I was talking about me."

Tom pushes his chair back, grabbing a last cookie. "You're not as smart as I thought, Susie. Dad likes you. Listen to the way he talks to you. Me, now . . ."

I look at my brother and try to separate the positive things he's said from the sarcasm in his voice, the hurt look on his face. "Tom, come on. If he likes me, he likes you."

Tom leaves the room without replying. I stay where I am. Thinking.

27
ON TOUCHING

WHEN I SEE TRACEE AROUND CAMPUS, SHE IS ALWAYS with three other girls, a clump. She is usually the one talking while the others watch her and smile. I have grown used to her split-second acknowledgment of me, her nod of recognition.

On the Tuesday before the next meeting I see her alone, walking through the courtyard. I am on a bathroom break; she is coming from the office. She looks me full in the face, and I am pushed back by the pain in her eyes, the flatness of the vivid brown. My impulse is to help, to save her. I raise a hand—why, I don't know. To wave? To stop her? Surely not to touch. Tracee shakes her head and hurries by.

I have been afraid of school mirrors. I never look in them when other girls are around, talking, laughing, shaking their long hair and applying lipstick.

In the bathroom now, I look at myself. I have not undergone any kind of miracle transformation. I am chubby still, round-faced, and my clothes don't suit me. But I have changed: I can see that. Maybe it is in the way I look straight into my own eyes, standing tall, not hunched. Or the way I wear my hair—back now, always.

I have decided that I like my face. It is my mother's face, and mine, and I am not going to hide it.

The door swings open and I restrain a flinch. It is Amber. She moves past me to a stall. "Don't go anywhere, Susan," she says as she disappears inside.

"I saw Tracee out there," I call, half embarrassed, curious about what Amber has to say.

"I don't want to talk about her," Amber says, and I turn back to the mirror, wondering.

When Amber emerges, I notice she keeps her eyes averted from the mirror. She washes her hands and turns to face me.

"I'm not coming back to Duffy's," she says. "I thought you'd want to know."

"You're not?" Out of nowhere, tears spring to my eyes.

Her expression softens. "You care. Why?"

I fold my arms across my chest. "I don't know. I like how you stand up. I watch you do it. You're strong."

Amber's face closes. "Not like I want to be."

"To me you are."

"They got it right, Susan. You are sweet."

I look at her to see the joke. But all I see on Amber's face is curiosity.

"I didn't think much of you when this thing started," she says. "I didn't think of you at all. You're something, though."

I am crying. I don't know what to say. I stand there and cry.

"Hey," Amber says. She puts her arm around my shoulder and gives me a half hug, half shake. I stand rigid and Amber releases me.

"It's not easy for you, is it?" she says. "Touching. Being touched."

I take a breath. Smile. "I'm getting better."

"Do you and Brendan ever . . ."

We lock eyes and laugh at the same moment, mine shaky.

"I know he's queer," Amber says. "But does he hug you hello, or kiss your cheek, or anything?"

"Yes," I say, drawing out the word, giving her a chin-down stare.

"Not my business, huh?"

"Not really." My posture shifts and for the first time with Amber, I feel relaxed.

"It's good you're friends with Brendan," she says. "A real something is better than sniffing after Randy Callahan."

I look at her, surprised.

"You make it obvious," she says, not unkindly, "the way you look at him. And you know that ain't going to happen. Right?"

"Right," I say, my voice tight. I wipe my hands over my cheeks.

"He's about as good a guy as he can be. Just stop thinking he's perfect. No guy is. Randy would tell you that himself, if he were honest."

"I don't think he's perfect," I say quickly.

Amber nods, solemn. "Uh-huh."

"Not much, anyway," I add, trying a smile.

She grins at me, and we laugh together.

After a pause, Amber looks away. "I checked out of my classes today," she says. "I'm flunking most of them anyway. I'll finish up next year at the continuation school."

"You should stay," I blurt. "In school. In the class. You're . . . I think you're a good person too, like Randy."

Amber reaches out to push back a stray curl. I let her. "You see what you want to see, don't you?"

I look at her. "Sometimes I'm right."

"You're as good as any of them, you know. Don't forget that."

"You either," I tell her.

28
THE HALF-FILLED CUP

I EXPECT TRACEE TO BE GONE ON WEDNESDAY, BUT she is here, arriving just behind Kale. She slides into the seat he is about to claim, the one closest to the door. Kale shrugs and sets up next to her.

"Amber has dropped out of Wayne High," Mr. Duffy says, "and, of course, this group."

No one looks surprised.

"I'm glad she's gone," Tracee says. "I tried to drop the group too. The principal wouldn't let me. He said I had to finish the program if I wanted to stay at Wayne High."

"You were so damn superior last session," Randy says. "I don't blame Amber for dropping."

Tracee shrugs. "That girl is a total whore. People like her shouldn't be allowed on campus."

"Amber isn't here to defend herself," Mr. Duffy says. "I think that's enough."

Kale laughs. "She wouldn't be saying that stuff if Amber was anywhere close."

"Shut up," Tracee says through her teeth.

"What about Justin?" Brendan's voice is quiet. "Should he be allowed on campus?"

Tracee shoots a glare at Brendan. "I don't believe things went down the way she said. Oh, I think he screwed her, but she wasn't some poor, pitiful victim. Not that girl. Justin's out of my life and thank God so is she."

My emotions shift. Loyalty to Amber makes me want to argue with Tracee. But despite her tough words, Tracee's eyes are hollowed and her voice is pitched high.

"Did you love him?" I ask. "Justin?"

"I don't know, Susan," Tracee says, her voice not so brittle. "I thought I knew him, and it was a lie. I thought I was smarter than that."

I hunt for words, aware of Brendan's eyes on me. "You can't always know everything," I say. "Why people act the way they do. Everything isn't always up to us."

"Us?" Tracee says, but the look in her eyes invites me in.

I shrug. "The girls who think they know it all?"

"Ah, conceited," Randy says. Brendan manages a grin.

Tracee groans. "Okay, all right. Next topic, please."

"This is the second-to-last meeting of our group," Mr. Duffy says. "Next week I want us to meet at Round Table Pizza downtown. My treat. What do you say?"

No one answers. I am thinking of Round Table—Mom and Dad's old stop for family celebrations—and picturing us there. I am used to this room and what happens inside but chilled at the thought of taking it public.

How can I eat pizza in front of everyone?

"Sounds great," Randy says, breaking the silence.

"Right," Mr. Duffy says, straight-up. "We have this session to get through, and I want you all to guide it. What do you want to say? Be bold. We're almost out of here."

"Amber dropping," Kale says. "And her trying to," he waves at Tracee. "That going to hurt you? With the principal, I mean."

Mr. Duffy sighs. "I'm afraid it might. This group was set up as an alternative to expulsion. Now, out of six students, one has dropped out of school and another has tried to leave the program. The administrators are trying to figure out the point of what we do here."

I hear the sadness in Mr. Duffy's voice. I look at him closely. Beyond the fat, he looks unhealthy, circles tugging his eyes down, face pale under a layer of sweat. I am sorry now that I did not get excited at his Round Table announcement.

"This is a great class," I say. "The best I've ever taken. I wouldn't have known Brendan without it."

A tiny insecurity drags at me as I look over at Brendan, afraid of what I might see: embarrassment, distaste, rejection. Instead he smiles at me.

"I got to know Susan," he says, "and she took the risk of being my friend."

"Uh, we don't all have to do warm fuzzies, do we?" Kale is slouched, legs outstretched.

"No warm fuzzies coming at you from this direction," Brendan says, smile in place.

"Krasner, give it a rest," Randy says.

"I don't know what you're putting on." Tracee's anger is a

shock. "You laugh as hard as anyone when Eddy Rogers does his fag act."

"You just have to push it." Randy stares at Tracee.

"It's the truth," Tracee says. "What's wrong is wrong. I don't want to hurt Brendan, but I'm not going to lie about my beliefs."

"I don't think being gay is wrong," I tell her.

"Susan, he's your only friend," Tracee says. "Wouldn't you say anything to keep him?"

An attack, but it is more important to answer than retreat.

"No, Tracee, I don't think it's wrong. It's just part of who Brendan is."

"She doesn't judge me," Brendan says. "Susan hears the stuff and keeps coming back. Most girls wouldn't."

I am staring at him. "You're the one. I can't believe how brave you are."

"What's it like, being Brendan's friend?" Mr. Duffy's voice is soft.

I hesitate. Brendan dips his head. "Go ahead, Susan."

I look around the circle, lingering on Kale. "I thought I had it bad at this school. It's nothing compared with what Brendan has to go through. I've heard more disgusting, obscene things walking around with him than I have in my whole life. Guys catcall him, ask him out, pretend he's coming after them. Why do guys do that stuff?"

Kale squirms. "What are you looking at me for?"

"You're the kind of guy who does those things. You know it's true. I'm not mad; I'm asking why."

"Same as I said with you." Kale won't meet my eyes. "Guys are looking to make each other laugh. Fags are tailor-made for it."

I feel the anger building despite what I've told him. "It's more than that. One time at lunch your friend Jason came up and punched Brendan in the back. He said, 'Suck my dick, faggot' and walked away. No one else was around, and Jason never even looked at me. Who was he trying to impress?"

"I don't know," Kale says. "I wasn't with him, okay?"

Mr. Duffy clears his throat. "Brendan, how do you feel when something like that happens?"

"Ashamed." Brendan's arms are folded, and he is looking down. "I know they're wrong, and I know they're assholes, but I still feel ashamed."

"I'm not going to do it anymore," Randy says.

"What?" Kale asks.

"Laugh at fag jokes. Or make them."

"Some of the stuff that goes on around him is too rude, maybe." Kale is staring at Randy. "But no one is going to convince me that fags aren't wrong. I mean, I'm sorry for him, if that's what he wants. But it's still wrong, what he does."

"I haven't done much," Brendan says. "You have me down as this raging queer, and I haven't done much more than kiss."

"Another guy?" The disgust in Kale's voice is absolute.

"Yes, Kale. Another guy."

I can't help but giggle. Tracee looks at me with almost as much disgust as Kale has shown. "Susan, he's wrong, and you're wrong for supporting him. I hope you'll understand that one day."

"I hope the same for you," I say, smile big. Tracee looks away, shaking her head, folded arms matching her crossed legs.

"I'm not signing the petition next year," Randy says. "If they ask, I'll tell them why."

Brendan regards him, then nods.

"Callahan, you're not saying it's okay, what he is?" Kale's eyes are narrowed.

"Yes, that's what I'm saying."

"It doesn't bother you that he . . ."

"No," Randy says. "It doesn't bother me."

"What are you in here for?"

Randy shrugs. "I guess it doesn't matter now. I'm doing time for Eddy Rogers."

"What?" Mr. Duffy looks alarmed.

"Rogers had too much stuff on his record already," Randy says. "So I took the blame."

"What happened?" Mr. Duffy's voice is flat.

"I was with Eddy and Justin one night at the school, and Eddy decided to break windows. The three of us were blasted. Me and Justin stood by while Rogers ran around with a two-by-four. A janitor was working late and saw Eddy's letterman's jacket, so . . ."

"That was you guys?" Tracee says.

I am amazed. I remember how angry Dad was at the destruction; nearly half the windows in the Humanities building had been smashed.

"Coach didn't push it when Eddy said I'd borrowed his jacket.

I figured I've done enough stuff I haven't paid for, I might as well take this one."

I look into Randy's blandly handsome face and realize that I don't know him at all.

"You understand this makes your participation here a joke?" It is the first time I have seen Mr. Duffy angry. "How many people has Eddy told? Or Justin?"

Randy sits up. "Hey, no one, Mr. D. Are you kidding? Why would they talk about this?"

"What about your parents?" Tracee asks.

"My parents think I did it. Justin, Eddy, and me, we made a pact not to tell. My dad's always thinking I'm better than I am. Now he doesn't know what to say. It was a relief, kind of, to slide so far."

"Randy, you're better than you think," I tell him. "That day in Axle Park, when we were in sixth grade, you—"

Randy is shaking his head. "I never saved your cat. My dad took the kitten from those guys. I didn't know what to say to them."

"I remember that," Kale says slowly. "Some cat we found in the park." He looks at me. "My brother and his friend took it out on me after Callahan's dad took the cat. You think that was fair?"

I don't know what to say to him. Or to Randy.

"Hey, everyone," Randy says. "About the windows. Keep quiet about that, yeah? I promised the guys I wouldn't say anything."

"I never knew how insecure you were," Tracee says. "Why can't you be your own person?"

Randy sighs. "It's official, Tracee. You are perfect."

"I'm not," she protests. "Stronger than you, maybe."

"Why are you in here?" he asks.

Tracee sits back. "Why should I confess? You just got through telling us how innocent you are."

"I confess to being there when Eddy broke the windows, lying to Coach, the principal, my parents, and Mr. Duffy." Randy smiles, and three months into our sessions, I still find him breathtaking. Despite everything and maybe because of it.

Brendan catches my eye. "Fun stuff," he whispers.

"You're just too cute," Tracee says to Randy. "And you know it, don't you?"

He nods, suddenly serious. "It works."

There's more to you than that: I know it.

Or do I only hope it?

"What happened wasn't my fault," Tracee says.

"Tell us," Randy says. "What does it matter now? Group's almost over."

"Amber's not here to rip you for it," Kale throws in.

Tracee looks at him. "True." She sits up straight, hands on her thighs. "Okay. I made Mrs. Luddington into a better teacher. That's why I'm here."

My stomach turns. Mrs. Luddington is an enormously fat woman who has taught English at Wayne High for decades. She is one of my touchstones, or used to be.

I am not as fat as her. I will never be as fat as her. I will never teach kids if I am fat.

"What did you do?" Kale's eyes are bright.

"She didn't teach." Tracee cuts off every word. "It was Honors English and she was showing movies every day. Any movie she could find. I mean, we're talking filmstrips about burro rides in the Grand Canyon."

Randy is laughing; so is Kale. I stretch a smile across my lips.

"I asked her for challenging work, and she blew me off. My parents called and complained to the principal. He said he'd talk to her, but nothing changed."

"Movies every class?" Kale says. "I would have loved it."

"I started documenting," Tracee says. "Taking notes in class, but not about the movies. I wrote a report on her incompetence and left a copy on her desk, with one to the principal and one to the school board. She changed after that. Back to our grammar text, essays, term papers, and all that."

"The class must have loved you," Kale says.

"I did them a favor." Tracee is fierce. "It isn't good for anyone to do less than their best."

Randy raises his eyebrows. "You're in here for writing a report on Mrs. Luddington?"

Tracee looks a little less sure of herself. "Not exactly." She looks at Mr. Duffy, who gives her nothing back. "We had an incident."

"An incident?" Kale is grinning.

Tracee touches her bracelet, caressing the initials with one finger. "Luddington gave me a C at semester. Pure revenge. My parents and I met with her and the principal, and she showed them all these F's in her grade book for the movie assignments I didn't do. Of course I didn't do them! I had A's on the assignments that mattered.

"She convinced the principal and Mom and Dad that my average was D. My parents aren't fighters." Tracee's lip curls. "I am."

"What did you do to Luddington?" Brendan asks.

"I met with her one last time to see if I could change her mind. Alone in her classroom after school. She wouldn't listen. She wouldn't even look at me. I started crying and she laughed. That's when I gave her a tap."

Kale's jaw drops. "You hit her?"

Tracee's back at him. "A tap. Nothing! A little . . ." She indicates a two-fingered slap, the kiss of a moth.

"Across the face?" Randy asks.

"Kind of," Tracee says, "but I doubt if she even felt it. Really, I barely touched her."

"You hit a teacher, and you're in here?" Randy shakes his head. "Man."

She looks at him, furious. "I did not hit her! Don't talk that way, Randy. You weren't there. You don't know what it was like."

I am seeing Amber's face.

"Luddington wanted me arrested! Kicked out of school. The way she told it, I was the criminal. But she stole that A from me." Tracee's eyes are glistening. "No one was in that room but me and her. I could have lied and said I never touched her. But I admitted the tap. That's why I'm here."

She glares at Randy, at all of us, chin down, arms folded. Her posture is eerily like Amber's under pressure.

It is piling on, but I have to say it. "Tracee, you shouldn't have been so tough on Amber. You should have tried to understand her."

Tracee shakes a finger at me. "Susan, she chose to be a slut, and she chose to use violence to solve her problems. I was provoked! I would never act that way unless someone made me do it."

"You're not perfect, are you, Tracee?" Randy says with some gentleness.

Tracee draws in a breath. "No. I'm not."

"No one is," Mr. Duffy says. "Try to give the same kind of understanding you want to receive. All of you."

We are quiet.

Mr. Duffy taps his watch. "We've hit the time, so—"

"Wait!" Tracee says. "Not fair. Susan has to tell what she did. Brendan too. And Kale."

"Round Table downtown, next week, three-thirty," Mr. Duffy says. "Now I know you'll all show up."

29
I Call

I FIND THE NUMBER IN THE JUNK DRAWER IN THE kitchen, the one that has never been emptied since we have lived in this house.

I cannot hit the numbers right away. I sit at the kitchen table, holding the phone loosely. My heart is thumping. I worry that I will not be able to speak even if she is there, still at the same number.

Benny meows and I jump up to pour him some food. Change the water. Drink some myself.

Then, standing, I punch in the numbers, the exotic area code I remember from five years ago.

She answers on the third ring. "Hello?"

"Aunt Cecile?" I say in a rush.

Only a moment's pause. "Susan?" She sounds so pleased.

"Yes," I say, gripping the phone. "Hi. I just wanted to say—"

"Oh, honey, how've you been? I've been so worried."

I expel the breath I have been holding. "I'm okay," I tell her. "I think I'm okay."

30
MEETING

ON WEDNESDAY I WALK INTO NO-MAN'S-LAND, THE athletic complex, just after school's out. Guys and a few girls mill around the doors outside the gym; inside I hear clanking from the weight room and glimpse a good half-dozen guys lifting. In the gym itself, the badminton courts are set up and the Wayne High team is filing in from the girls' locker room to practice.

I am nervous but try not to show it, keeping a measured pace. I am headed for Dad's office.

I see him behind the shatterproof glass, in the alcove between the boys' and girls' locker rooms. The door is ajar and I pause outside, watching him. Dad is staring at a clipboard, leaning back in a battered swivel chair, his desk inches thick with papers, including school dittoes, old *San Francisco Chronicle*s, his playbook, and class lists.

I clear my throat, waving when he looks up. "Hi, Dad."

Dad stares at me, rocking his chair back straight. "Susie. Is something wrong?"

"No." I shift my books to the other side. "I was wondering if you could give me a ride somewhere."

"Oh," he says. We look at each other.

"Can I come in?" I nod toward the other chair in the room.

Dad glances at his clipboard then sets it down. "Sure. But you said you need a ride?"

I take in the musty smell of the office, the newspaper articles tacked everywhere, the trophies dusty on the shelves. The picture of my mother behind his desk.

"Maybe we could talk first," I say, sitting across from him, leaning around to close the door. I notice a schedule calendar tacked up behind the door. It is identical to the one at home, Dad's conferences and meeting times blocked out for the month of May.

When I turn back, Dad can't seem to keep his eyes on me. His gaze shifts over my shoulder, to his left and out the window, back to his desk. He fidgets in his chair.

"I wanted to let you know I called Aunt Cecile," I tell him. "Yesterday."

"She called you?" Dad looks at me, brow furrowed.

"No." I lean toward him. "I called her."

Silence. Dad shrugs. "Why?"

She's my aunt. She's your sister. I missed her. I need an adult to talk with.

I pick the easiest answer. "I missed her, Dad. She was happy to hear from me. She said she misses us. She'd like to visit sometime, or we could go there."

He is shaking his head. "That's not going to happen."

"Why?" I ask, angry. "Why do we have to be so alone?"

"We make our own lives," Dad says. "I've managed to do that, and so has Tom. You need to get out more, to live."

"That's what I'm trying to do," I tell him. "That's why Mr. Duffy's class—"

Dad's face closes. "I've told you not to mention that class. It's over soon, isn't it?"

"Yes," I say. "It's over soon."

"Good." Dad looks at me, really looks at me. "Time enough to forget that whole incident."

He is angry, I see. Anger he hasn't shown. "I embarrassed you. With the truck."

"Of course you did. You know you did."

I start to answer him. Dad holds up a hand.

"It isn't worth discussing. You're a good girl. I know that. I appreciate the way you take care of the house. Your grades. The way you stay out of trouble . . ." He trails off. "That's what we have to get back to. That's why the only thing to do is forget this mess."

I feel the Nothingness closing in. The time Before the Truck.

"I can't go back to the way I was before," I tell him. "I'm awake now."

"Awake? What are you talking about?" Dad glances out the window. A muscle-y boy and a muscle-y girl are passing. His face relaxes, looking at them.

"Damn it," I whisper, "can't you listen to me?"

He frowns in my direction. "What's the problem? I paid for the kid's truck, and I found a way for you to work off what you did. What more is there to say?"

"You never asked me anything about that day. Aren't you curious, even?"

Dad sighs, shaking his head.

"Why can't we talk about things?" My voice is rising. "Why can't we ever talk about Mom?"

He stands, gathering a handful of papers off his desk and stuffing them into his clipboard. "Where do you want me to drive you?"

I slump in the chair. "Round Table Pizza. Today is Mr. Duffy's last class."

———

DAD IS DRIVING TOO FAST AROUND WAYNE'S BACK-streets. We pass Brendan on the way.

"How did things work out for that kid?" Dad asks, tilting his head back in Brendan's direction. "He was in the group with you, right?"

"Brendan and I are friends," I tell him, twisting my fingers in my lap.

Dad brakes at a mini-intersection. "Tom mentioned something about that. I'm glad you had someone to talk with in class, but you need to back away from him."

"Would you rather I spent time with no one?" I am looking down, but my voice is firm. Dad stays where he is until someone honks at him.

Punching the accelerator, he says, "You're not getting me. I don't think you understand about Brendan Slater."

I am clammy in the icy, air-conditioned SUV. "His being gay, you mean? I understand. Brendan is my friend. I'm lucky to have him."

We've reached the shopping center where Round Table is located. I ask Dad to circle the block.

"Forget the gay thing," he says, slowing through the residential neighborhood. "The kid manipulated you into vandalizing that truck. I know you wouldn't have done it on your own."

I see Dad's mouth quirk and we catch each other's eye.

"Susie, you almost gave me a heart attack." All at once he is laughing. "I get a call from the principal that my daughter trashed some cowboy's pickup? This is not funny. It's not funny."

"I know." I laugh with him, relieved.

"Okay. I'm listening. Why did you do it?"

I hesitate. The truth is complicated, and I don't want to lie to him.

Dad squints at me. "I don't know how to handle this. Give me a clue, huh?"

I think about it. I gesture to a parking spot near the end of the block. Dad pulls in.

We sit for a moment. Then I turn to him. "You don't really want to know, do you?"

Dad takes off his Wayne High Wildcats cap and tosses it on the dash. "I'm not the best parent. That was your mom's department. I don't know what to say to you."

I am surprised he has said that much. "It's her birthday soon," I say, choosing the words carefully. "I was thinking maybe we could see where she is . . . where she was buried, I mean."

"She's nowhere," Dad says. "I had her cremated. The funeral home still has the ashes, as far as I know."

I draw in a breath, my hands tightened into fists.

"I'm sorry," he says, his voice hoarse. "The last time we talked,

Cecile let me know where I came up short as a husband, a father, a brother. I can't say she was wrong about any of it."

"Dad, it isn't like that now. Aunt Cecile just wants to see us. She's not mad, if she was before."

He shakes his head. "I can't be around anything that reminds me of that time."

That's us, isn't it? Tom and me?

"I need to talk about Mom once in a while," I say. "The way it is now, it's like she never lived. I don't see how it makes you feel better to forget her."

Dad holds up a hand. "I haven't forgotten her. I never will."

We are quiet again.

"I've lost weight. Have you noticed?" I ask, each of us staring down the leafy street.

He turns to me. "You look fine." Shocking me, Dad reaches over to touch my hair. "More like her every day."

"I'm not an athlete," I say with a shaky laugh, looking away from him. Dad removes his hand, but I can still feel it.

"I don't expect you to be an athlete." The gentleness in Dad's voice brings me back. "You're built like your mom."

"I'm fat," I say immediately, cringing at the bitterness in my voice.

"Well . . ." He sighs, and I am tense, thinking the conversation is over. "Nina—your mom—worried about her weight too."

"I thought maybe . . ." I close my eyes and take a breath. "That, you know, it might be easier with us, you and me, if I weren't so fat."

Dad is quiet. I turn to him, blinking hard, determined not to cry.

"When have I ever said anything about your weight, hon?" he asks finally.

I scan my brain, my experiences. Mostly, Dad is not there. But I remember one time.

"At Denny's, right after the truck," I say. "You told the waitress I should have a Diet Coke instead of a regular one."

"I may have," Dad says. "I'll have to take your word on it. I'm sure I was ticked off at that point. You don't know how much I had to do behind the scenes to smooth things over on that truck."

"Is it the money?" I say. "Because I can pay you back. I want to pay you back."

"No." Dad is shaking his head. "It isn't the money. You knocked me out of alignment, Susie. I have to keep moving. That's what I do. You made me stop and think."

The tears spill over as I absorb his words. I grab some tissues off the dash.

"That's what you wanted from this, isn't it?" he says slowly.

"I guess so," I tell him. "Yeah." I press the tissues against my eyes. Faster than I would have thought, I gain control.

"What you're doing at the track," Dad says, his voice careful, "I've been meaning to tell you, I'm proud to have you out there with me."

"You are?"

He nods. "Nice to have my daughter for company instead of the team kids running punishment laps."

I am confused until I remember Randy's story about the windows. About the things he got away with. "Those boys, that day, who were jogging with you . . . ?"

"Rogers, Wright, and Callahan. Those were makeup laps. I usually have 'em out there after school."

"But Randy is . . ."

"He's the best of them," Dad says. "I was glad when I heard he'd be in the group with you."

I recall Randy's kindnesses. "You didn't tell him to be nice to me or anything, did you?"

Dad looks off down the street. "Of course not. I'm glad to hear that he was."

"I guess we should get going," I say, suspicion tugging at me, mixed with something else, a realization building.

Dad cares.

"Right," he says, relief in his voice, and he starts the car.

We drive to the shopping center in silence. As we swing into the lot, I see Brendan leaning against the railing in front of Round Table. Anyone who didn't know would think he was a jock, just a guy, some cool, quiet kid.

Dad pulls into a spot a few spaces down from the restaurant.

"Thanks for the ride," I say, giving him a quick smile.

"Susie." Dad holds me with a look. "I heard what you said, all of it. I still want you to cut that kid loose after today." He tilts his head toward Brendan, who is looking away from us. "He's not a safe friend for you. He'll only hold you back."

I am shaking my head. "Brendan isn't the problem. It's the other guys who are. The ones who make petitions against him."

"The petition is a shame," Dad says. "You know, I'm the one

who approved the medical waiver for that kid so he wouldn't have to take PE. The mother brought in some bogus excuse and I signed off on it."

"I wish you'd told the guys they couldn't do the petition instead." My voice is quiet. "I wish you'd tried to stop it. And his name is Brendan, not 'that kid.' "

Dad grimaces. He tightens his hands on the steering wheel.

"And I love you, Dad," I tell him, my stomach tight to absorb his rejection.

He looks at me quickly. "Thanks. I feel that way too. About you."

We nod at each other. I look to Brendan, who is watching us now.

"I better go," I tell Dad. "Thanks again for the ride."

He catches my wrist. "If you want to see your aunt this summer, I'll send you. Tom too, if he wants to go."

"Really?"

Dad nods.

"Thanks," I say. "I'd like that."

"When should I pick you up?" He is brisk now, grabbing for his hat off the dashboard.

"I'm going to hang out with Brendan afterward," I tell him. "I'll walk home. It's not that far."

Dad hesitates. Then he tips his cap. "Have a good time, Susie."

31
ROUND TABLE ROUNDUP

BRENDAN NODS AS I APPROACH. "EVERYTHING OKAY?" he asks.

"Sure," I tell him. "Just talking with my dad."

Randy is just inside the door, at the end of the ordering line, as Brendan and I enter the restaurant.

"Hey, guys," he says. "Thought I'd see if I could get us a free pizza. My cousin works here."

I scan the room but don't see the others. One of the two large corner tables is taken over by a group of sheriff's deputies, while middle-aged and older women sit in pairs and alone at the smaller tables throughout the restaurant.

Brendan and I claim the other round table with our books and backpacks. I see the reflection of the jukebox lights around the corner, and I know the video-game alcove is just beyond that.

"Want to play some music or something?" I ask Brendan.

"Sure." He pats his pocket. "I have change."

In the mix of country-and-western, heavy metal, and light pop, I see a few oldies: the Beatles, the Doors, and my dad's favorite,

Creedence Clearwater Revival. We lean over the machine to choose.

"Well, what have we here?" someone says behind us. I jump like someone has hit me with cold water. Brendan is more controlled.

"Here," he says, giving me a handful of quarters. "Start feeding these in the slot and I'll punch in the songs."

"Punch you, boy," another voice says. Heavy. Deep. Familiar.

Following Brendan's lead, I pretend nothing is wrong. The coin slot is on the side of the machine, and I reach around to stick in a quarter. Someone pushes by and I fall to one knee, bracing myself against the wall. I look up and see Brendan cornered as squat, muscular Eddy Rogers punches in a tune.

"I'll take this one," he says. "Queerboy. You got yourself a real cute girlfriend."

You're a real cute girl. . . .

I freeze. He is the one.

"Hey, fatty." Eddy is hanging over me now. "Stick another quarter in the slot." He turns back. "You hear that, Justin? Stick it in the slot. Stick it in the slot. Come on!"

His friend, Justin Wright, takes up the chant.

"Stick the quarter, bitch!" Eddy directs.

I stare at him. My hand closes tighter around Brendan's money. "No," I say.

Eddy makes a grab for my hand. I pull free, recoiling from his sausage fingers.

"Leave her alone!" Brendan shouts out of a wind tunnel, and

everything stops as a Led Zeppelin tune comes blasting out of the box. Then somehow I am up and Eddy is on the floor.

I stand with Brendan as he faces Justin, who is taller than him, more muscular, more handsome. But Brendan is the strong one, holding steady as Justin fidgets.

"I don't even hate you, Justin," he says, "if that's what you want. I have a feeling you do enough of that for both of us."

Eddy gathers himself and springs up next to Brendan. He shoves him hard against the jukebox. I cry out, and Eddy stares at me.

"You're the coach's daughter," he says, a mean smile playing on his lips.

"Yeah. I am." I pause to catch my breath. "So tell me, when are we going out?"

"Huh?" Eddy glances at Justin, who looks away.

"You've been calling me. Checking my dad's office calendar, right, so you don't get him by accident?"

"You're crazy," Eddy blusters.

"You ask me out over and over. I finally say yes, and you never call back. Are you trying to hurt my feelings?"

"Whoa, Susan," Brendan says.

I keep focused on Eddy. "Call me again," I say softly. "Please call me again."

"Shit," he says, attempting a laugh. He turns to Brendan. "What's your deal, fag? Is she your protection?"

Randy appears behind Eddy and Justin. He pushes left, pushes right, and then he is alongside us.

"Callahan," Eddy says, a warning in his voice, "we got this under control."

"Looks like it's over," Randy says calmly. "Whatever it was."

Eddy takes a step forward. So does Randy.

They face each other, Eddy's chin tipped, Randy expressionless. Then, like that, Eddy's posture shifts and he is defeated.

"What are you doing here?" Eddy asks.

"Having pizza with friends," Randy says easily.

"Friends? Not these two." A smile plays along Eddy's lips. "Really, who you here with?"

"Susan, Brendan, and a few other people." Randy is unsmiling.

I watch Eddy's eyebrows rise almost to his hairline. Randy nods to Brendan and me.

"C'mon," he says. "Let's get some Cokes."

After the three of us have our sodas, we head for the table Brendan and I have claimed. On the way we pass Eddy and Justin, set up near the jukebox.

Randy stops. "Did you get a chance to pick the songs you wanted?" he asks us.

"Let's not push it," Brendan says.

"I want to push it," Randy says.

Brendan looks away. I feed the machine and punch in the songs. Randy talks quietly with Eddy and Justin.

Beatles music should cover the silence as we sit down on the circular benches, but it doesn't. Randy leans his back against the wall and stares into space. I am next to him, room between us. On my right, Brendan fiddles with his cup, rubbing his thumbs on the cold, sweating plastic.

"You didn't have to do that, Randy," he says. "I could have handled it myself. Susan was holding her own."

The Doors click in with "People Are Strange." I look down to hide a grin.

Randy focuses. "I should have done that six months ago. Longer."

Brendan and I stare at him.

"All kinds of shit happens while I stand and watch. So much has gone on just because I've been afraid of those two."

"You were scared of them?" I can't believe it. "You're so much better than they are. A million miles above."

Brendan's knee hits mine under the table. I blush. "Sorry."

Randy grins. "I'm not so nice all the time, Susan. Take my word on that."

"You took the blame for Eddy, on the windows," I say slowly, realizing. "If you hadn't, he would have been in Mr. Duffy's class. Not you. I'm glad things worked out the way they did."

"So am I," he says.

We nod to each other in a kind of understanding between equals.

"I asked Amber to come to this," Randy says. "I think she should be here."

I smile at him. "You think she'll take you up on it?"

Randy gestures to the door. Tracee, Amber, and Kale are headed our way, so widely spaced no one would know they are together.

"Scootch, Susan." Tracee's voice is tight. I am leaning back against the wall, like Randy, and she wants the space between us. I figure her anger is for Amber, but still I don't move.

Tracee's scowl shifts to a smile. "Please?"

I shrug, leaning into the table to let her by, wishing I had the nerve to say no. Not yet.

Amber takes the spot next to Brendan. She looks good, face scrubbed, hair in a ponytail. "Hey, girl," she says to me.

"Hey, Amber." I am shy, remembering the last time we talked.

Kale plops down next to Amber. "Where we putting the Fat Man?"

"Don't call him that," I say, staring across the table.

Kale holds up his hands and I wait for the zinger. "Whoa. Whatever," is all he says.

Tracee gestures. "He's in line."

Mr. Duffy sees us looking and waves.

"I think we should do something for him," Randy says, glancing toward the line. "Just something to let him know . . ."

"Let him know what?" Tracee says. "The class was pathetic. A disaster."

"Tracee, what would have happened to you without it?" I ask. She doesn't answer.

Amber shakes her head. "I dropped out, so . . ."

"But the class helped you, didn't it?" I ask.

"Sure, why not?" I see the doubt in her eyes.

Even Brendan is looking at me confused.

"Why don't you write something?" Kale tosses at me. "You're smart. Write something, and we'll all sign it."

I am thinking. "Okay. But we all write it, and we all sign it."

"Hi, kids," Mr. Duffy calls as he approaches. As one, we move in around the table until a space appears to accommodate him. "Half pepperoni, half veggie sound good to everyone? I ordered an extra-large."

"Hey, Mr. D," Randy says. "My cousin works here. I got us an extra-large pepperoni for free. He's charging it off as a school donation."

"Terrific," Mr. Duffy says. "Two pizzas; maybe we'll get some leftovers out of it."

A tall, sweaty kid with a brown buzz cut brings the first pizza over while Mr. Duffy and the others are getting their drinks. Randy and Brendan help themselves while I get busy setting napkins around.

Back at the table, Mr. Duffy urges me to take a slice.

"I'm a vegetarian, mostly," I tell him. "I'll wait for the other pizza."

I make my Diet Coke last as I watch them eat. Even Tracee is picking away.

"Hey. Everyone." Brendan sets his third piece of pizza down half finished. He looks at me almost apologetically. "I want to say what happened. Why they put me into Mr. Duffy's class."

My stomach curls, and I am glad there is nothing in it to react. Brendan is opening his mouth.

"Kale," I say, talking fast, "we trashed your truck. Brendan and me."

Everyone turns to stare at me. I can't read Brendan's expression.

Kale is frozen, a long strand of cheese dangling from the slice of pizza he is about to inhale. "What?"

"Remember? Back in February, when your—"

He stops me with a look. "I know when it happened. You and Slater? No way."

I am remembering the fear I used to hold. "I'll let Brendan tell the rest."

Please let me take this with you. Don't take it alone.

Brendan regards me, then looks around the circle. "I had to do something. It was Kale or me. I slashed his tires, yeah. I didn't slash myself. I didn't slash him."

"I am not believing this," Kale says. Slow. Icy.

"I wanted to hurt him," Brendan says. "I felt like I'd go crazy if I didn't do something. I went for his truck. He's yelled stuff at me from that truck enough times. At Susan too," he adds.

I nod, relief flooding through.

"One day I took some stuff to school," Brendan says. "Spray paint. A fish knife. A hammer too, wasn't it, Susan?"

Another nod. I feel my pulse pounding in my throat.

"Go, girl!" Amber is laughing.

"Hey!" Kale breaks off from Brendan to stare at her. "They slashed my tires and sprayed my windshield and broke my mirrors off and keyed my truck. You think that's funny?"

"Your truck's fixed," Amber says. "You said the school took care of it."

"That don't matter! It's still wrong, way wrong." I see the frustration on Kale's face, the helpless anger.

"It hurts," I say to him, my voice cracking. I clear my throat. "What you've done to us, it hurts. What you do to everyone, to everything that can't fight back."

Kale is red-faced. He is shaking his head. I draw back as he leans across the table, pointing at me. "I sat there and listened to your sob stories, and you knew!"

"Kale." Mr. Duffy lays a hand on his arm. Kale shakes it off.

"Why aren't you talking to me, Kale?" Brendan says. "Or are you planning something later?"

Kale works his mouth. I see a muscle jump in his cheek. He looks at Mr. Duffy.

"I think it's important to admit what happened between you and Brendan." Mr. Duffy's authority is clear, even with a sky-high pile of crunched napkins in front of him.

"It ain't the same." Kale's voice is flat. "I pulled some shit. Me and a couple of my friends, yeah. That ain't the same as going after a guy's truck."

"Nothing's the same," Brendan says. "You tell me. What was I supposed to do?"

Everyone is quiet as Randy's cousin appears with the second pizza. My stomach rumbles above Creedence in the background.

"Take some," Mr. Duffy urges. I nod, pulling a piece free, watching Kale.

"You were supposed to quit school," Kale says, glancing at Brendan, past me. "How you held out so long, I don't know."

"What did you do to him, Krasner?" Randy asks.

Kale is tearing a napkin apart. "We started with phone calls." Brendan nods. I flush, thinking of my brother.

"We got his schedule and graffitied his desk in all his classes. It was easy."

"You are sick," Tracee says.

"Hey, at least I didn't hit him," Kale shoots back. Tracee flinches.

"You shoved me a couple of times," Brendan says. "Knocked me into lockers and stuff."

"Jason did more of that than I did; admit it!"

"Like Susan said, it all hurts." Brendan stares at Kale. "After a while, you don't break it down. You just hate."

"Why did they put you in the group, Kale?" I ask.

He looks at me. "I wanted to get Slater on his library job. The guys thought it was too risky, so I went in by myself. I was writing stuff on one of the back tables when I felt these cold fingers on my neck. It was the librarian. I never heard her coming." He shrugs. "Next thing I know, I'm in Mr. Duffy's class."

"What were you writing when she caught you?" Randy asks.

Kale doesn't answer.

"It was 'Die, faggot, die,' wasn't it?" Brendan takes a sip of Sprite.

"Yeah," Kale says. "I wrote that. We wrote it everywhere."

"Did you mean it?" Brendan enunciates every word.

Kale looks at him. "It don't sound good now, but yeah, I guess I meant it."

They hold the gaze, and Brendan nods. "Thanks for being honest."

"Kale," Mr. Duffy says, "the important thing is, would you do it today? Would you write those things about Brendan today?"

A long silence. My fists are clenched in my lap, nails cutting into my palms.

"No, I don't think I would," Kale says. "Still don't make it right, what they did either."

I release the breath I have been holding. "I can't do this on a lie," I tell them. "I didn't do Kale's truck. I loved Brendan for what he was doing, but I wasn't part of it."

"You were a part of it," Brendan says. "When I looked at you that day, I knew I wasn't alone."

"Thanks," I tell him after a pause. "That's what I wanted you to see."

"You're both crazy," Kale says. "Did she mess with the truck or not?"

I take a bite of pizza, chew and swallow. "Not, Kale. Stop shouting stuff from that truck and maybe no one else will be tempted."

He frowns at me, at Brendan.

"I have faith in you," Mr. Duffy says. "In each of you. I'm proud of the way you've learned from each other. That's what I'm going to take away from this. Tracee, how about you?"

"I learned that my boyfriend was cheating on me," she says. "I guess I have Amber to thank for that." She speaks normal volume and I see Justin watching her from across the room. He taps Eddy on the chest and the two leave the restaurant.

"I did you a favor, Ellison," Amber says.

"Maybe you did," Tracee says. "I haven't decided yet."

We are quiet around the table. Amber and Tracee watch each other. I jump into the silence.

"This class taught me I could say stuff to people and it wasn't that horrible. Even Randy Callahan." I smile. "Even Kale Krasner.

I used to think I wasn't real. Or they weren't. I don't feel that way anymore."

"Susan." Kale hesitates over my name. "Nothing I did to you was personal. I didn't know you were even thinking about me."

"I was thinking about you. Way too much," I tell him. "I hope that's over now."

"I ain't going to bother you," he says. I think I see someone at home in his eyes.

Tracee laughs a little. "Susan, don't take this wrong, but this class showed me you were real. You and Brendan. It was good for that, I guess."

"I already knew you were real," Brendan says. "All of you. I even bought bumper stickers to let you guys know the way I'm going to remember you."

He ducks into his backpack and pulls out a zippered vinyl folder full of stickers.

Tracee looks at me and I shrug.

"Okay, Mr. Duffy," Brendan says, handing him a slick sticker.

Mr. Duffy reads it, laughs, and holds the sticker up for us to see: "Practice senseless beauty and random acts of kindness."

"Amber!"

Amber squints at hers. "You kidding?" Brendan shakes his head, and she grins, displaying the sticker: an eagle feather curving around the legend "Warrior women rule!"

"Kale." Brendan's voice is careful as he hands him the bumper sticker: "Cowboy Country" spelled out in yellow block letters on a black background.

Kale reads the words over, then nods. "Thanks," he says, like he is waiting for the punch line.

"Randy, here's yours."

" 'Straight but not narrow,' " Randy reads out loud. "That's great. I should put it on my Mustang just to see what everyone says." He hesitates. "My uncle, I'll show it to him next time he comes up."

"Whatever you want," Brendan says, looking past him. "Tracee, you're next."

"I can't wait," she says, reaching out. I read the sticker at the same time she does: " 'Christians aren't perfect, just forgiven.' "

Tracee half laughs, half groans, holding her sticker for the rest to see. "Brendan! I never said I was perfect."

Brendan pulls the last sticker out of the folder. "Susan, now you."

I take the sticker gingerly, holding it out to read. It is home-made, with black letters in script on a white background.

Tracee tilts her head to read with me. "Well, that's nice, I guess. Shakespeare, isn't it?" Brendan nods. "But what does it mean?"

"Susan, read it out loud," Randy says.

" 'Sweet are the uses of adversity.' " I hold it up for them to see. My eyes are blurred with tears, but my hands are steady.

Letter to the Wayne High School Board
 cc: Mr. Roy Duffy, counselor
 cc: Mr. Theodore Grottigen, principal

We, the members of Mr. Duffy's after-school counseling
group, want to thank Mr. Duffy and Wayne High School for
giving us a second chance. We ask that Wayne High continue
Mr. Duffy's program next year. Here are the reasons why:

Mr. Duffy's class is good. It's cool how people talk.

Kate Krisner

The counseling group is beneficial. Students discuss the
consequences of their actions and counsel others with
different problems. The learning is achieved across
boundaries.

Tracee Ellison

I think Mr. Duffy's class should go on. He let us talk and
stayed out of our way. More school should be like this.

Amber Hawkins

Mr. Duffy's class made me want to be a better person.

Randy Callahan

I might have disappeared without this class.

BRENDAN SLATER

Me too.

Susan Callaway